The Target

T.D. Deinstadt

Copyright © 2023 T.D. Deinstadt

All rights reserved.

ISBN: 9798389876712

DEDICATION

For Brody, Cole, and Lucas. You were all so excited when I told you I was writing a book, so much so that you came up with enough ideas for ten books in various series. I can only hope that you'll like this one.

CONTENTS

	Preface	Pg 1
	Prologue	Pg 3
1	Isolation	Pg 6
2	I'm Where?	Pg 54
3	Hourglass	Pg 69
4	A Break	Pg 94
5	The Government	Pg 119
6	Escape	Pg 138
7	Homeless	Pg 164
8	Jim	Pg 184
9	Surprise	Pg 211
10	Shadows	Pg 244
	Epilogue	Pg 276
	About the Author	Pg 281

ACKNOWLEDGMENTS

For my mother Christine for all my stuff she puts up with and my nephews Brody, Cole, and Lucas for all their encouragement while I was first struggling to write any books let alone this series. All the love and thanks!

PREFACE

The Tattoos appear when you hit puberty. Your first one matches the tattoo your mother received when she became pregnant with you. Then over your lifetime other tattoos appear and they stay with you permanently. They predict what will happen to you, both good and bad. But if you receive a skull, it's over. You die. Nobody survives - nobody. I received my skull almost a year ago, and although it was a close call, I did survive. With the help of a good friend and some cops. Not only did I survive, but the skull disappeared. Then, in the same spot, it was replaced - by a target. I'm positive it's not a good tattoo. After all I wasn't born with a four-leaf clover on me - luck is no friend of mine.

PROLOGUE

Christmas had come and gone with Lynn and the little whale. My parents had enjoyed their cruise arriving back home to discover the changes. The trial was pending for Mark and Annie. The divorce had been a cakewalk for Lynn. The lawyers that Jim had brought to the house found all the evidence needed for her to receive all the assets and full custody plus any extra restitution she wanted to claim. Not that it mattered. Lynn had everything she needed to go forward with life. It turned out that Mark had been hiding millions from her. Now every dime was in her name. All she wanted was to be a good mother and keep her son safe and happy.

My name had been all over the news after the arrests. Images of me with my skull tattoo were everywhere. With all the attention on the upcoming trial, I had been getting more and more unwanted publicity. Jim had offered to let me work from home again although I declined his offer. I can't blame him for that. All the cameras had been on him during his divorce because of Annie. The business had taken a hit because of it. He was positive we would recover but I wasn't so sure. He'd begun taking steps to make Annie give up her shares so that she would no longer be associated with the company. If the stocks took another hit because of the trial, the company would end up bankrupt. All I wanted was for all of this to be over.

The thought of having my space to myself again with no one waiting to ambush me for a photograph was a massive craving now. There'd been threats directed towards me from people that had been Annie's "friends" after the divorce debacle. More from Mark's contacts as well. It seemed that no matter how hard I had worked to save myself from the destiny the skull on my arm created, the attention it had drawn made me a target. Which explained my newest tattoo.

1

ISOLATION

The cameras began flashing in my face the second I stepped outside my home. I couldn't handle it anymore. They were constantly at me, clicking away even though there was no real reason for it. It was getting worse and worse as the trial approached. Vultures. No one needed my picture at this point. It was everywhere. This was just plain old harassment now. There was nothing that the police could do either. I'd spoken to both Dutch and Andrews. So long as they didn't come on to my personal property, they were doing nothing that could be construed as illegal. They'd even investigated stalking laws – the problem was that every few hours the people would change out, so it wasn't any one person long enough to qualify.

I got into my car. I'd spent some money to get the windows tinted with the hopes that it would make it harder for people to get an image of me. It had worked to some extent. Now people would step out in front of my car to get a picture through my windshield. I kept changing up which directions I took to get to work. The grocery stores I used were on a random rotation depending on which route I took. It still didn't stop the problems though.

Today, as I pulled into the grocery farthest from my home hoping to pick up some basics, I could see a crowd already gathered in the parking lot. At first it seemed like they were talking to each other about something in a cart in the middle of the lot. I parked and got out of my car grabbing the reusable bags as I closed and locked up. Walking forward while trying to skirt the crowd was difficult but I managed it. The yelling wasn't hard to make out.

"This is our neighborhood grocery store – if you don't live in the area, you shouldn't be allowed on the property. It's different if you are in the area for shopping or on your way to or from work. You picture predators are just gumming up the parking lot for those of us that need to get groceries. I'm going to complain to the manager about you!" A large man stormed off in the direction of the store. I tried to discreetly follow in his wake.

The distinct "there she is, quick" tipped me off that I hadn't been as discreet as I'd hoped. I bolted into the store. I'd learned early on at this store that if I started at the farthest end, away from the registers, I could hit every isle I needed. Then straight into a line. Self-check if at all possible. Normally I'd avoid having to check my own items – the light, polite chit chat with a real person had always been welcome in my life. The problem was that now it took a considerable amount of time to go through a regular check out. Time was of the essence when I knew I'd been spotted. My list suddenly cut down to half of what I had wanted.

At a full run I managed to get everything that was most important in less than ten minutes. They still managed to find me and follow me. The flashing lights drew more attention than I already had. The people from the neighborhood were beginning to give me dirty looks. I became pinned in a circle of cameras. They weren't allowing me to move in any direction. I dropped my basket and began to shake. My breathing began to restrict, and then it was like I couldn't breathe at all. Tears slid down my cheeks. I became dizzy and my vision began to fade. Suddenly an arm reached out and began to shove the cameras away from me. The man grabbed my basket, my bags and my arm and pulled me out of the circle. He continued to pull me along until I was in a back hall somewhere. I hadn't been able to keep track of where I was going. A paper bag was thrust in front of my mouth.

"Just breathe. In and out, nice and slow. You're having a panic attack. It's ok. I'm here to help you. I want to keep you safe." A large man was squatting next to me. He had black hair that was beginning to recede. Dark brown eyes were set in a chocolate face. "It's ok. You can trust me."

The sympathy – the first I'd received in ages – was too much for me. I broke down crying and hyperventilating. Time seemed to stand still. I'm not sure how long it was before I began to breathe normally again. My weeping slowly stopped. I was exhausted and everything hurt. I'd been sitting in this position on the floor for too long. The strange, kindly man helped me to get into a chair. When he saw that I was calming down he began to speak to me.

"My name is Brogan. Frank Brogan. You've probably heard of me. I'm a journalist. I came to see if I could do a proper sit-down interview with you when I saw you being surrounded. Damn paparazzi. They don't seem to understand that they can really do some harm with their behavior." His face contracted into a wince of complete and utter disgust when he talked about what he'd seen.

"Thank you. I've never had a panic attack before. I hope that I won't ever have one again." My throat was sore, gruff, and raw as I spoke.

"No need for thanks – no one should have to go through what you are. I have a safe place you can stay in if you're interested. I can arrange to have food delivered there. It might be best to get away from the whole situation."

I eyed him warily; I didn't know this man although he seemed kind. But dealing with the paparazzi again was something I didn't feel able to do. I took a leap of faith.

"If you'd asked me this morning, I would have said you were wrong and that I was doing ok. Let me make a couple calls. I'll get my business partner to gather some things from my place and meet us in the lot."

Frank nodded and stepped out of the

room. When the door opened, I could see the store manager talking with the police. I'd have to give my own statement before I'd be allowed to leave. Before calling Jim to explain what was going on I pulled up the browser on my phone. It took no time at all to find out that Frank was legitimate. He had been in the journalism industry for at least 15 years and had his own interview show. His face was all over his website, he was who he said he was. I wasn't willing to do an interview, but I'd explain that to him in a few minutes. If he didn't want to give me a safe place to stay, then I'd talk to Jim and see what arrangements he could make. I dialed and waited for him to pick up.

"Hey, I sent you a copy of the stock info. It looks like we are finally beginning to recover from the publicity of the trial date. Once the heat backs off you, everything will get back to normal and the business will go great guns again." Jim sounded downright cheerful at the prospect.

"I had a problem, Jim. Look, I went to the grocery and was basically surrounded by cameras and people, and I couldn't move. I had a panic attack. A journalist, Frank Brogan, managed to get them to back off and he and the store manager have popped me into the office here while the police clear off the paparazzi. Frank says he has a place I can go where no one will be able to find me and he can arrange for food. Can you come to meet me? I don't think I can go home and get things or even move my car without running into another group."

"Of course. I'll get my car dropped at your house and then I'll drive yours home from the store. Make a list of what you need, and I'll use my key to pack it up. I can meet you and Brogan wherever you want." Jim seemed stunned by what he'd heard but inevitably wanted to find a solution. Frank came in as I hung up.

"Jim's coming to get my car and he will pack my stuff for me. He's willing to meet up and make sure I'm covered."

"Sounds like a pretty good friend. You're lucky to have one. Ok I need to make a couple calls so that there are supplies delivered and the place is ready for company. The police want a word with you about what happened. Once they are done the store manager has asked for a list of what you were planning on getting. He said that he'd pull it from the shelves and run you through the system back here. That way no one bothers you and it causes less disruption to the other shoppers."

I'd never be able to show my face in this store again. I began making my lists as I stepped out of the room and into the waiting arms of the police. Faces I hadn't seen before. That was a first in a long time. I had come to know a lot of them. They took my statement and assured me that they would do what they could to keep the lot clear but once I was on the streets it was public property and there was nothing more they'd be able to do.

Once I'd finished the list for Jim I texted it to him. The store manager handed me a notepad and told me to write out what I needed. Since I was going someplace where I didn't know the supply situation of the basic necessities, I ended up with three carts worth of food, drink, hair care supplies, etc. I was told to go wait in the same back office while the manager wandered off with the list and a couple of his employees to pull what was needed. Frank was sitting in one of the chairs on his phone when I entered.

"I know honey. I promise I'll make it up to you. I certainly didn't think that I'd be walking into this situation when I went to speak with her. She needs my help. If all goes well, I'll be back by 10. Then I promise I'm all yours for a weekend. No following a story. Just you and me and that list of chores you keep for me. Ok – love you too." A smile ran across Frank's face as he hung up the phone with a shake of his head. "My husband Sean. We were supposed to be having dinner with his parents tonight. It's the third time I haven't been able to make that dinner. If I'm being honest, I'm not fond of my in-laws so I don't try very hard to attend these dinners."

"Sounds about right," I started to laugh since that was an issue I knew I would never have. Not because I didn't believe in marriage or because I've seen the messy results when relationships ended. After all, my parents had been together for nearly forty-five years. No, I didn't want to share my space. I liked being alone. I liked not having to constantly work on a relationship or be reminded every time I opened my eyes that I was in a fight with someone that I couldn't avoid. Then there's constantly watching and doing things I didn't enjoy just to make the other person happy. Call it selfish if you like but I think it would have been more selfish of me to marry and then refuse to compromise to accommodate the other person. Changing like that is just not who I am.

"He keeps this list of things I need to accomplish on the weekends or during vacations – you know the typical list. If I can knock off a couple of things like painting the spare room or hanging the curtains, then Sean should feel I've done what I can to make amends. So once I get you settled you won't be able to get a hold of me for a couple days. I'll call you first thing on Monday morning to touch base." At that moment Jim texted that he was in the store and ready to take my car. Frank and I went out and I handed off my keys. Jim looked concerned but didn't say anything. He glanced at Frank and gave him a nod before squeezing my hand and leaving.

Frank kept giving us odd glances as Jim left. I knew he'd probably seen all the tabloid articles. There had been a few that stated we'd gotten together before his divorce and that we'd framed Annie and Mark to simply get rid of the two of them. It didn't help that their lawyers were taking a similar tack. It was around this moment when the store manager came back with everything bagged up and told me I could come to the front to pay. Frank followed; the total was a little on the painful side, but it would be worth it. I'd have a nice quiet weekend alone again. With a lot of time to bake and cook, which I must say, is one of my favorite pastimes.

I followed Frank out to his SUV, and we began loading things up in the back. The paparazzi were still there but they were carful not to step on the grocery store lot and to stick strictly to the sidewalks. I was still getting dirty looks from people who were trying to get in and out of the parking lot. It seemed everyone knew who it was that was causing the issues. Once settled and buckled into the car Frank began to drive. Every few seconds he would look in the rear-view mirrors and then swap lanes and make a turn.

"Where are we going?"

"At the moment, nowhere. I'm trying to lose the tails we picked up at the grocery store. Don't worry I've had experience with this. I wasn't always behind a desk," the last was said with a smile and little chuckle to himself. "Text that friend of yours and give him this address."

The paper he pulled out of a cupholder was a little tattered and had some kind of drink stain on it. I recognized the name of the village. It was about three hours outside of town. A tiny little place with a general store that supplied all their food and clothing needs. If you wanted fresh bread, there was a bakery that also had a coffee shop and gas station attached. A sheriff's office shared its building with the only restaurant and a little art gallery. The village itself only had a couple hundred residents in it. If you took in the surrounding countryside that number grew to around a thousand. I typed the address in to google and discovered that this particular home was about an hour on the far side of the village. Very isolated with no near neighbors. I'd truly be alone.

It didn't scare me – I'd always wanted to live out in the country, have some acreage where I could put in a large garden and more than a couple of fruit trees and bushes. My mother had been thrilled when I'd pulled all the grass out of my backyard and put in my garden. Mostly because it gave her fresh fruit all summer. There was always too much for me on my own. Now I would get just a tiny taste of my dream of privacy.

"So, it's going be a long drive. How many more people do we have to lose before we start heading in that direction?"

"A couple more turns, and we should have lost the last tail. Then I'm going to head to the far side of town and loop around the outside to get us going in the right direction. That way, if someone does figure out the direction I'm driving, there's several hundred exits for them to investigate. It's doubtful that they will know about this house. It belonged to Sean's sister. She got her skull when she was just 20. She passed a few days later. The house went into a group holding for use by the whole family so there is no one person's name on it. Sadly, nobody in the family has been able to face going there. I go out and use it when I'm working on a project or as a safe house for people like you. People that need a place to hide out for a short time."

The Target

I felt awful for Sean's sister. To have gotten a skull that young and never really getting a chance to live. Still Frank was right. If no one really used it and it didn't have his or his husband's name on it, I should be safe there. It felt like hours before we were on the edge of town slowly working our way along the bypass highway. Jim texted to confirm if the place had Wi-Fi or if I'd need a mobile hotspot set up and to find out what the cell service was like in that area. He was glad that he'd get to meet us there – I could tell that something was just not sitting right about the whole situation for him.

"Is there Wi-Fi and cell service?"

"At the house? Yeah, there's both, though it can be spotty when there's bad weather. The landline is stable now. The family insisted on having it brought in and a cell tower added to the edge of the property. Sean's sister couldn't reach anyone after a fall and ended up dying from internal bleeding. No one knew until a few days after some storms had passed through the area."

I felt like a monster poking at what was obviously still a sore spot for Frank, but I needed to know. I didn't want to be so alone that I'd be unable to contact help if some random person suddenly showed up. We both fell silent as I texted the information to Jim. The city cruised by my window. We finally made it past the second to last exit, and we began to see more trees and bushes along the roadside. Frank pulled off the last exit pointing towards the right.

"If you need to stop for food or to use the washroom now is the time. After the next gas station there's no place for the next three hours. That's when we will be in the village. You don't want to stop there right away either – less chance of someone remembering you and saying something. So, we're looking at about four hours of no stops."

"We should pull off. I can fish some snacks out of the bags and use the washroom." I had known that the drive would be a long one but that long without the option of stopping for a break was a little daunting. The only time I'd done a drive that long without a stop was when I had been a kid. When dad had his vacation time, he and mom would bundle Lynn and I up and take us to visit relatives ten hours away. They always woke us early, around four in the morning, and then they'd make us use the washroom before hustling us to the car where we'd go back to sleep while they drove. We'd wake up again around 7:30 and have a half hour to become conscious of where we were. Then they'd find a place to stop by 8:00 for food, a washroom break and a stretch.

After that there'd be regularly scheduled stops every two or three hours. It was different on the way home – still the same wake up time but there was a ferry ride at the beginning of that trip so we would be wide awake through the morning drive and then after lunch we'd usually fall asleep and wake when we stopped for dinner. It was a long trip but if we hadn't gone to visit the relatives then we would never have seen them. I can count on one hand how many times in my life that my relatives had made the journey to visit us.

Funny what goes through your mind when you aren't constantly running in survival mode. I hadn't thought about my relatives in years. My cousins would occasionally visit us but for the most part it was just my immediate family that I spent time with. Perhaps that was why I preferred being alone. There had always been times in my life where I'd simply had no one because my family or friends were busy, so I learned to entertain myself. I came wide awake with a start when I felt a hand on my arm. When had I dozed off?

"We're here." Frank had already unloaded the stuff from the back of the car onto the front porch of the farmhouse. It looked like the porch only covered part of the front of the house. I could see one side also had a little porch area as well, probably with a side door. The house was minty green colour that had a weathered gray look to it, with white trim and black shutters. It was on the small side and surrounded by ancient looking willow trees whose bare branches swayed slightly in the breeze. The sky was a slate grey, and the clouds were heavy with snow. I could see Jim's car parked on the other side of us. He must have packed my stuff and driven like a crazy man to be here already. Frank opened the door to the house and turned on a couple of lights while Jim made his way over to me.

"Look I don't trust this at all. We don't

know this guy and yeah, he's a legit journalist but that doesn't mean he can be trusted. What's his agenda?" Jim kept glancing at Frank as the bags were being slowly ferried off the porch into the house.

"I know but right now I don't have much of a choice. You probably saw what it was like at my place. I haven't had a good night's sleep in weeks. I just need somewhere that no one can find me. This fits the bill. I have my phone so I can keep in touch with you that way. Frank is basically dropping me then heading home to make up with his husband. I won't hear from him until at least Monday."

"My gut says he can't be trusted so just be careful, ok? I picked up a second phone and added it to my account for emergencies. It's fully charged and tucked in with your computer stuff. If he asks about it, you can say that it's your work phone." Jim lifted my computer bag out of the trunk and handed it to me, he then pulled a couple of suitcases out and carried them towards the house. Frank was waiting for us in the foyer.

"Ok I've checked, and it looks like everything is working. The heat can be a little temperamental so before I go, I'll haul some wood in for the fireplaces. There's a couple down here and a couple upstairs. I've stayed here when the heat's been off and not been cold at all. I ran the water in the kitchen, and it came up clear, but you'll probably have to do that with all the taps. I haven't been here since last fall when I was working on a story." Frank was eying Jim up with a clear question on his face.

"Frank this is my friend and business partner Jim. He brought me some clothes and my work stuff so that I'll have something to do while I'm here. Jim this is Frank." A brief handshake showed how little either of them trusted the other.

"Let me take these upstairs for you Dawn," Jim shoved his way past Frank with the suitcases and began heading up the stairs.

"He seems nice, I guess. So, the living room is to your left. The dining room is on the right and at the back is the kitchen with a door to the side of the house. Don't forget to lock up at night. I doubt anything will happen but if someone does track you here then you'll be safer from them inside the house. I doubt you'll want to be outside though – not with that storm coming in." With that Frank walked out and off to the side of the house where a little open-sided shed stood. With how dark it was beginning to get I couldn't tell how much wood was stacked there. Jim came down the stairs and without a word walked out to his car, started it, and left. I'd call him later and make sure he made it home ok. I was a little surprised that he hadn't offered an alternative to staying here. Jim had become "take charge" when my life had been threatened. He simply made arrangements instead of letting me dither about the choices I needed to make.

Frank stacked wood by each of the fireplaces while I went upstairs and began unpacking. At the top of the stairs there was a small hall, the first open doors revealed two bedrooms each with a fireplace and a bit further down the hall a third door held the bathroom with an old clawfoot tub next to the window. My cases were on the bed in the room to the right. I walked in and started unpacking my electronics. A small dresser had enough space for me to set my laptop. The side table had just enough space for my spare phone and a glass of water for the night. There was a little glass lamp there as well. The fireplace took up most of one wall. The double bed took up the opposite side and across from the door was a single window with little white lace curtains. Not much privacy but since the house was in the middle of nowhere, I guess you wouldn't worry about people seeing you change. A creak on the stairs alerted me to Frank's presence.

"If you're all set, I need to head out to get in front of that weather." A glance out the window revealed that it had started to snow lightly.

"Yes – I think I have everything. Thank you so much for this Frank. You have no idea how much I appreciate it." I walked him out of the house. He waited to hear me throw the deadbolt before he went to his car. I watched his headlights move up the driveway. When they were no longer in sight I turned and went into the kitchen. The stove was very old, it looked like an Aga that had been converted from wood to gas. There was lots of counter space. A fridge that looked like it was from the eighties was in one corner next to the exterior door. I double checked the bolt on it was turned. I was starving! I realized I hadn't eaten the snacks I had pulled at the beginning of the drive, mostly because I'd fallen asleep once we were back on the road.

Though the bags had been brought in nothing had been put away. As I stuck an ice cream tub that was beginning to drip into the freezer, I thought about what I could do for a quick and easy dinner. I had all the ingredients for my fancy grilled cheese. I'd even included some wine and chips on the list. A perfect, easy dinner. The house felt like it was still on the cool side so after all the food was put away and before I started cooking, I went through the house and lit the fires. The two on the bottom floor weren't open fireplaces, they had stove inserts. That made me feel much better. An open fire had to be carefully tended but as long as the insert and chimney had been cleaned out in the last few years, I shouldn't have too much chance of an accident occurring.

The dining room was small but serviceable. I could easily set up there to do some work when I wanted. The living room only had a small tv mounted on one wall. I didn't see any disk players or cable boxes. Just under the tv was a small open shelving unit with lots of Knick knacks and on one side the Wi-Fi router with a little piece of paper taped to it. It appeared to be the name and password for the unit. I could always hook up my computer with the spare HDMI cable I kept in the bag. That would give me something to watch. I wandered back to the kitchen.

The Target

I had to open several cupboards and drawers to find everything I needed but once I had, I started to work on my dinner. A thick sauce with some gouda in it was used in place of the butter. More cheese into the French bread slices. Everything went into the pan. Once it was melted there was enough of the sauce that I could thin it with some milk and use it for dunking my grilled cheese.

I flashed to the first time I had made this in front of Annie and Jim. Annie had been so disgusted at the idea of using something that wasn't tomato based she didn't want to be in the same room while I ate. Jim had been game to try some. Afterwards he'd begged for the recipe. I grabbed the bag of chips and the full bottle of wine and headed into the living room. Setting everything down on the coffee table I popped back up to the bedroom to retrieve my laptop and cords. Once I'd set it up, I began scrolling through my various streaming services trying to find something to help keep me calm.

I had finished eating while watching an old tv series. I had stoked up the fires to make sure they'd last through the night and decided to go to bed as soon as the episode I was watching was over. But the stress of the day caught up with me. I woke up wrapped in the blanket from the back of the couch with the bright light of daybreak streaming in. It had snowed heavily all night and the sun was reflecting off of the snow making it seem much brighter than a normal day. The tv had turned itself off sometime during the night and my screen saver was flashing away on my computer. Dishes were still strewn across the coffee table and the partly eaten bag of chips had fallen on its side to the floor.

I went upstairs after sitting the dishes in the sink to soak. No dishwasher here. A relax in the bath seemed like a good idea but before I did that I knew that I needed to clear the snow away from the house at least out to the woodshed. That way I could keep the house warmer. Rummaging through my bag it looked like Jim had thought to pack some of my winter clothes. I bundled up in a sweater and my thickest leggings. I didn't have a proper jacket or gloves with me, so I went down to the foyer. There was a little cupboard under the stairs and after digging around I came up with some gloves and a hat. Far at the back was an old winter coat – it wouldn't keep me warm for long but hopefully shoveling would.

Looking out of the front door there was no shovel visible. Out the side door was an old snow shovel. It may not last with heavy use but with luck there might be another shovel in the woodshed. I began working my way there. The sun was fully up and with the clear sky and I could feel the temperature dropping. My nose and cheeks had begun to freeze. Only a few more feet until the shed. It was packed to the roof with wood so at least I wouldn't freeze to death. Luck was no friend of mine though – no extra shovel. It would take me hours to clear the driveway using that ancient spade. I would wait until it was warmer to start that. Since I was already cold it made sense to put the shovel by the front door and then bring a few loads of wood over. I could stack it on the porch and not have to worry about going out to the shed in the middle of the night.

With that done I went back inside. I was so sore. It felt like every muscle had begun to seize up. The fires had gone out. Knowing that out in the boondocks a cold house could mean cold water I started the fires again. Once I was sure they wouldn't go out I went upstairs and picked out some clean clothes, then ran a bath. I checked the time and it turned out to only be 8:00 am. I'd missed several messages on my phones. On my normal phone Jim had sent a couple of messages asking me to call him as soon as possible. When those had gone unanswered, he'd texted the emergency phone. The last message said that he would be coming out to the house if I hadn't texted back by nine. I sent him a message saying I was fine and that once I'd had a bath, I'd call him.

I crawled into the hot water and felt like my legs were on fire. Looking at my thighs I could see the redness from the cold burn. I'd have to be more careful. I couldn't afford to get sick or need help until I got the driveway cleared. That was a multi-day project. I laid there for a good forty-five minutes.

I finally felt warm. I got dressed and decided I needed to add a couple extra layers. There was a fresh text from Jim saying he'd be waiting for my call. I took the phone down to the kitchen and popped my headset in while I did dishes and made some breakfast.

"What happened? Why didn't you answer my messages last night?" Jim's voice was filled with a deep fear that I hadn't heard since he left college and had to tell his parents that he was planning to start his own business using his trust fund and not get a well-paying, nine to five job.

"I had to build the fires, put the groceries away and I had barely eaten so I made dinner and tossed a show onto my laptop. Then I passed out. My phones were both upstairs next to the bed, where I had intended to sleep. This morning I got up and had to shovel the path to the woodshed so that I could bring more wood in." I was scrubbing the sauce pot and began to feel a little lightheaded. Sticking the pot back into the sink to soak longer, I began to dig around for a bowl.

"My house and our offices were broken into last night. I told Dutch and Andrews where you were and what happened yesterday. They both promised to keep it off the record, but they were worried. My security system went off and I think it scared the burglar away. Would you mind if I stayed at your place for a couple of days? I'm having a security team stay at mine and at the office."

"Of course. I'd feel better about my house not being left empty with all those people looking for me." Cereal into the bowl with some milk, I went into the dining room to sit and eat. "Are you ok out there? It sounds like you really slept hard although I'm sure you needed it. Don't worry about work. With Andy's help I've been doing fine handling everything. I'm thinking that we should promote Andy – you could bump up to the open CEO position. I know - not the time to talk about it - but just think it through. We can decide later."

"I'm fine. The driveway is hip deep in snow though. It's going to take days to dig out assuming we don't get another dump of snow. I should be able to clear it with that crumby shovel in the next three days. I'll think about the position. For sure we need to promote Andy – he's doing way more work than any assistant should. Draw up the paperwork and I'll look it over." Jim seemed calmer after hearing that everything with me was ok. We chatted for a few more minutes and he promised to send the promotion paperwork to me that afternoon.

After hanging up I went back to the kitchen and started scrubbing that pot again. From the window over the sink, I could see out across the yard towards the road that curved around to connect to the driveway. A plow went rolling past. Everything was just so quiet. Normally I loved being alone. I always had something to do. But today it was not that easy. I started to mull over everything that happened the day before.

A knot began to build in my stomach. There was something wrong. Something that I was missing about the cameramen. I just couldn't put my finger on it. My phone began to buzz in my pocket.

"Hello?"

"Hey Dawn, it's Frank. I just wanted to let you know that I've arranged to have the driveway cleared when snowfalls like this happen, so you don't need to worry about it. Usually, they also do a section so that you can get to the woodshed too. I told my guy that Sean and I had lent the cabin to a friend that was just out of a bad relationship. That way no questions."

"Thanks Frank. I did find a shovel and dug a path to the shed this morning. I hauled some extra wood to the porch so I can just grab from there."

"Great. Since I have you on the phone maybe we can talk about your interview. I was thinking I can come on Monday and sit with you. I can record the audio and we can discuss a time when you can come on my show. That way you know the questions I'll ask, and we can prepare you."

"Look Frank I don't want to go on tv. I don't like the attention. I don't want to talk about how my ex best friend and ex brother in-law tried to murder me because I accidentally stumbled on their affair. It's going to be bad enough when the trial starts."

"Well, I'll come past on Monday, and we can talk about it." Frank hung up without letting me protest again about not wanting to do the interview.

The sound of a large machine outside the house drew my attention. I stayed behind the curtains as much as I could while snow was being removed. When the guy was done, he got out of the cab and carried a couple new shovels over to the porch. I ducked down so I wouldn't be seen. He didn't knock, just left the new shovels by the door with the old one and then left. The day seemed to be crawling by. The rest of my day was spent tending the fires, making food, and watching shows on my laptop. Eventually Jim sent me the paperwork and I made a couple adjustments – Andy deserved more money than Jim had listed. After sending them back there was nothing left to do but wait for the time to make dinner. I fell asleep on the couch again.

It was the odd flashing that woke me. Night had fallen. The curtains were a thin sheer material that let the light in through the day. I wandered over to the window. The light was coming from the woodshed. It was a regular flashing as if it was timed. A car was parked in the driveway. I grabbed both phones and tucked them into my pants pockets. Shrugging on my borrowed coat I slipped out of the door and towards the shed.

Arriving there I could see a camera on a tripod standing pointed at the house. Every once in a while, it would take a picture and when it did the flash would go off creating the light I'd seen. Once I was close enough, I grabbed it, but the flash went off right in my eyes causing me to go blind for a few seconds. During that moment I heard something behind me and tried to turn only to have a hard object make contact with my head. I dropped to my knees and struggled to look around. A sharp pain ran through my neck and then everything went black.

2

I'M WHERE?

I was strapped to a table when I woke up. It looked like a lab room of some kind. Bright white walls bounced the overhead lights around. There was no window. The table felt like a hospital gurney. The bindings had a soft woolly cloth that wrapped around my wrists, ankles, across my chest, legs, and waist to prevent chaffing. There were brown leather belt pieces that kept them tight and then looped around the bars of the bed. It was on the cool side but not cold.

I could move my head. Looking down I was dressed in a hospital gown. I had no sense of time or any idea how long I'd been there. An IV in my hand made me think that it had been at least a day. Probably longer.

"Ahhh, awake at last. For a moment I thought that you'd stay in a coma. I'm Doctor Robbins. Welcome to my lab." The man that stood before me was in a doctors' lab coat with a suit shirt and pants underneath. He was tall, at least from the position I was in he looked tall. Brown hair that was slicked back and shot through with grey. He had a thin frame and looked like he'd been a heavy smoker at some point. His teeth had that yellow look to them. He was making notes on his clipboard while I tried to get my mouth working. I struggled against the restraints, wanting to sit up.

"Sorry but you won't be sitting up just yet. If you comply with my instructions, then I can let you sit up while you eat. The bump on your head has healed nicely. I'm sure you're wondering how long you've been here. I brought you here five days ago. It's currently Wednesday. I had to put you in to a medically induced coma just to be sure there was no lingering damage from the hit to the back of your head." Robbins held a cup with a straw to my lips and I did manage to get some water into my mouth and down my throat. I was still raspy when I started to speak.

"What happened to me? Who hit me

and what did they stick me with? Where's my stuff?"

"You were hit on the back of the head and given a heavy sedative. As for who hit you, that would be me. You see you're unique. A person that has not only survived a skull tattoo, but had it change. It's fascinating. What's different about you? I've given you a full physical and done all kinds of blood testing on you. There's nothing abnormal. Nothing to explain how you did it." The look of sheer frustration on his face spoke to the truth of what his testing turned up. "Why you? There must be some kind of reason – maybe something in the brain that lights up differently from a normal person."

He picked up a controller by the side of the bed and proceeded to press and hold a button that moved the top of the bed to a sitting position. Once I was fully upright, I was a little more uncomfortable, the straps felt like they were pressing into my skin. Robbins left the room through a door that I hadn't been able to see before. There was a mirror on the same wall. Other than that, I could now see little cabinets in the mirror that were on the wall behind the bed. A sink and a counter sat on the cabinets. They were all stainless steel with what looked like plastic fronts that would prevent breaking but allow a person to see the medications being kept in them.

Robbins came back in the door with a little trolly. On the trolley was a tray filled with food. From behind the bed he pulled a stool, then sat and began to feed me a broth that tasted like a mix of vomit and tomatoes. I tried to protest but every time I opened my mouth, he would put more food in. He was going to discover very quickly that I had a sensitivity to tomatoes. It made me violently ill to eat them. He managed to get an entire bowl in to me. I sat and began to feel the telltale cramps that came before the food would start to come back up. Robbins didn't seem to notice the distress I was experiencing. He'd begun eating his own lunch as he began asking questions.

"When did you first get your skull tattoo? The exact date please – it's not mentioned in any of the articles. Remember if you don't comply you don't get the privilege of sitting upright or eating food, I can give you all the nutrients you need to stay alive through that IV." Robbins leaned forward to catch any words that may have been too quiet to hear.

Bad idea. I opened my mouth and began to projectile vomit all over him, the trolley, and myself. Not that I cared about him and the trolley of food. Robbins fell off the stool and tried to roll away from me, knocking the trolley over at the same time. I got a minute or two between bouts of illness to gasp for breath before getting sick again. He stood staring at me from across the room. The horror on his face as he realized what he was now covered in would have made me laugh if I hadn't been vomiting at that moment. Instead of trying to find a way to help me he fled the room leaving the door open. As the last of my stomach contents hit the floor and I was able to breath freely again I leaned back and looked to see that there was another room beyond the one I was in with all kinds of machines, it looked like there was an MRI in there, I could see the table with the edge of a large circular piece near one side. I felt disgusting. I was in desperate need of a shower. Somehow, I knew I wasn't going to get one. I managed to locate a clock above the door, and it was over an hour before Robbins returned.

"I assume you're finished now. I'm afraid I'll have to put you under again while this mess gets cleaned up." With that he walked over and shot something into the IV access from a syringe. I began counting backwards in my mind and I last remember thinking the number 4 before I blacked out.

The Target

* * * * *

When I woke everything was clean and I'd been washed. A set of shivers ran down my body. I was no longer in the lab room. There was a large machine over me, and I was strapped to it. This must be the MRI machine I'd seen through the open door.

"Glad that you're back again. I think this time we'll start with the machine. You need to be completely still while it scans." Robbins voice was tinny and kind of metallic. He must have been speaking through an intercom system. I was still feeling groggy when machine around my head began to spin up. It's a good thing that I wasn't claustrophobic. The machine ran for far too long in my opinion. My sense of time seemed to be completely messed up, probably due to having been drugged at least twice.

"Excellent. Now I'm going to come in and bring you back to your room."

Since my head was strapped down this time, I couldn't see anywhere around me just the ceiling which was briefly replaced by Robbins face. The straps were removed from my head. A stiff board was slid beneath me. This was tipped one way then slid on to the gurney. A second set of straps was put on to me and the first removed before the board was pulled out. I was wheeled into the lab again.

"I tried to tell you that I was allergic to tomatoes, but you kept putting food in my mouth without letting me get a word in. "I'm sorry for your shirt and the mess." There, at least now he knew why I became sick. With luck he wouldn't hold it against me.

"Hmmm, that certainly explains a great deal. I won't hold it against you, and I will add that to my list of information about you. Now I have several questions and you will answer them!"

"I'll do my best, but I don't know much about it. I can't recall the exact date that I got my skull. I have it in my phone along with a voice memo to help me remember the information I needed for when I get called at the trial. That's one of the reasons I don't want to do interviews – I have a terrible memory of the incident."

"I see. I do have your phones and I will power them on. Give me your code and I'll pull up the memo and get as many of my questions covered as I can. Then if I need to clarify anything I can ask you."

"Sure, the code is 4372. It's in the built in voice memo app. I didn't name it since it's the only set of recordings in there."

Robbins left the room. If all went well Frank would have reported me missing. Or Jim would have when I didn't answer either of the phones. Someone would realize that they could be pinged and find me.

Luck is no friend of mine. Nobody came. I only saw Robbins when it was time for food. This time no tomatoes. He wasn't interested in talking to me and didn't bring his dinner into the room. I was quickly fed and left after the bed was placed into the sleeping position. I had time to think while lying there. I'd seen Robbins before I just couldn't place where. The soft stuff on the straps came up to the middle of my hand. As I lay there in the dark, I began pulling at it with my nails. It took a long time for the first thread to break but once it had I was able to start pulling the fluff out of it. I tucked the fluff under the edge of the bottom sheet of my bed. There was a lot of twisting to reach it, but I couldn't leave any evidence of what I was doing where Robbins would find it.

Days passed. I'd done some serious searching of my unremarkable memory while I pulled out the fluff around my wrist, thread by thread. I finally realized where I'd seen Robbins before. He was the cameraman that I'd seen in the store parking lot. Also there had been a time last year when I was at the hospital that I'd seen him – he hadn't stood out in my mind since he hadn't been the one treating me. That's why I had started worrying about those memories back at the house. Cameraman and doctor, those memories just didn't jive, and my subconscious knew it. And I kept working on the straps. If I could get enough of the fluff removed, then I could get an arm free. Once that was done it would be nothing to get out of here. Robbins made appearances at every meal but never stayed or spoke to me. I felt like I was beginning to go crazy. I had figured out the timing on the meals and began to pull the fluff out in between the visits. There was almost enough space if I squeezed my thumb into the center of my palm to slide my hand out. It would hurt but it could be done.

Tonight. After dinner I'd pull out the last of the fluff I needed gone and then I'd get free. There was only an hour until then, now I just needed to bide my time. I suddenly felt the burning on the palm of my hand that indicated the beginning of a new tattoo. I couldn't turn my hand over properly to see what it was. I'd have to look at it later. Patience has never been my strong suit, but I didn't have a choice this time. If I wasn't patient I'd get caught – then I'd end back up in a coma. Even if I just found a working phone line so that I could call the cops. Anything to get out of here.

3

HOURGLASS

Robbins didn't come to me at dinner. When the door opened I felt relieved and then very confused. Was this all some kind of game? I couldn't believe what I was seeing. Frank stood there. With the trolley full of food. He walked in and sat himself down on the stool. He had a look of guilt on his face. I could feel tears stinging their way out of my eyes and down my cheeks. My throat tightened up with my desire to scream at him over this betrayal.

"I should apologize but I'm not going to. Let me explain. This has far more to do with my husband and my marriage than you think. You see the doctor you know as Robbins is my husband, Sean. I told you about his sister Jenny. That part was true. The interview was supposed to give us some answers about why you were chosen to survive when Jenny didn't manage to. You refused. Sean felt that it wouldn't have answered any of our questions anyways. He thought there had to be some kind of biological component."

"You set me up. You offered me shelter, safety. Just so that you could imprison me in a lab and run tests on me? How can you even live with yourself?"

"Look I met Sean through Jenny. She was an intern with me. We became great friends and when she found out that I didn't have anywhere to go for Christmas one year she insisted I join her and her family. Sean was just out of med school back then. I was still travelling around covering wars and earthquakes. We hit it off, started seeing each other whenever we had time. Eventually we got married. Jenny was thrilled. She'd become my assistant by then and we travelled around together. Life was so good."

"Sure – it's always good until it isn't any more."

"Yeah well – Jenny and I had gone to Mexico City to cover some election protests that were going on. Violent stuff but we shouldn't have had an issue. I turned my back on her for just a second and she was gone. I contacted the police there and the government in hopes that someone would help us locate her. It was months before she was found. Still alive…. and pregnant. A skull tattoo had shown up on her neck. We brought her to our house and tried to get her to tell us what had happened. All she said was that when the tattoo showed up she was dumped on the streets and then the police found her."

"That's horrible but what does it have to do with *kidnapping me?*" I was beginning to let my frustration show through. I felt bad for Jenny – it's a terrible thing she'd gone through but from what Frank had said before she had passed years ago. There was nothing I could do for her or anyone else that had gotten a skull and passed away.

"The sounds of the city caused her to have all kinds of mental breakdowns while she was with us, so we set her up with the house in the woods. We checked in with her every day and Sean would come and spend his days off from the hospital with her. He's the one that found her. I may have fibbed a little when I told you that she'd fallen and bled out internally. She did fall and bled out internally but there was some evidence that she'd done it purposely. Our sweet Jenny had set up a ladder at the top of the stairs and thrown herself down them. Sean was never the same after that. He became obsessed with finding people that had skull tattoos and tracking their actions.

Eventually he became convinced that these tattoos aren't natural, that someone or something is assigning them to us. I've been interviewing and researching. There's no record of people surviving a skull tattoo but there are a number who were recorded in the past as having them that just disappeared off the face of the planet. No record of names, family, where they lived, nothing. Just a random report here and there of a person having one and then gone."

"You've certainly explained why you wanted to interview me. What's happened though, has gone way too far! I'm being held here. Against my will. Sean has experimented and used medical procedures on me that I never consented to. Do you honestly think that this would solve anything for either of you? Nothing any of us do will bring Jenny back. I'm pretty sure the only reason I survived my skull tattoo was because I have never believed that they dictate our lives. I refused to bend over and let the bad things happen to me. Attitude changes everything." I refused to speak to him any further. I turned my face to stare into the mirror and ignored Frank for the rest of the meal. As he stood in the door before leaving, he looked back at me and there was a deep sadness there.

"We've gotten all we can from your phone and from the medical procedures. There's only one thing left – Sean's going to give you a full lobotomy tomorrow. He thinks that he saw a structure in your brain that's different. He wants to study it up close. So, this is goodbye."

Frank hadn't bothered to put the bed down into the sleeping position. All the lights turned off and I could look through the mirror for a moment before the lights in the other room went out. I waited five minutes just to be sure that no one was going to come back and change the bed position. Then I started pulling the last of the fluff out. It didn't take too long. Once my arm was free, I was able to reach the strap across my chest then my other arm. Legs and ankles last but most important. I pulled the IV out of my hand and searched around in the dark for something to stem the blood flow.

My legs felt like jello at first as I tried to stand. I collapsed to the floor; every joint seemed to ache. Thankfully I was angry enough about my situation that I was able to push past the pain and force myself to move around. Time seemed to stop for a while. Once I was stable on my feet, I headed straight for the door. Frank hadn't turned any kinds of locks on it. I opened it and was able to get a full view of the other room for the first time. There was a distinct glow from machines that were in sleep mode. I was able to see the new tattoo on my palm. An hourglass with the sand equally distributed between the top and the bottom. It looked pretty fancy – the supports between the top and bottom of the hourglass were little dragons. Stretched across the bottom was a tiger. It looked like it was preparing to pounce at some unseen animal. It wasn't a four-leaf clover, but I hoped it meant I would be able to get out of here if I was patient enough. I began to explore the room. To the left of the door where the mirror was in the other room was a window confirming that I was likely observed from here without my knowledge. Under the window was a desk with all kinds of notes papering it. I went to it with the hope that one of the drawers had my things in it.

Luck was no friend of mine. All I found were the notes about some abnormal brain structures and the possibility that this was what caused the tattoos and my survival. Copies of my medical information were there as well. The far wall had shelves filled with all kinds of chemical bottles. Behind the machines was a door. I slipped over to it as quietly as I could. There were no sounds coming from the other side. With a little breath I tried turning the handle. It was unlocked!

I opened it a crack and peeked through hoping that I wouldn't see anyone waiting there. It also had no window, and the lights were out. There was some type of equipment in there as well. It gave a small amount of light in the darkness. I could see the outline of a couch and a countertop to one side with a door just beyond that. The door had a window in it which let some light come through. It was like a fire door you'd see in a hospital. Beyond it was a stairwell which was lit up. The rest of the room had a table and tv mounted on the wall. Next to the tv was a solid door I can only assume was the washroom. I quickly padded across the room since it was unlikely my things were there either and looked into the stairwell. When I couldn't immediately see anyone, I slowly opened the door. No sounds other than myself. I was at the bottom of the stairs. To my right was the first set of stairs and on my left was a small closet. I opened it up and found a stack of linens and on one of the shelves a little box with my name on it. When I opened it up, I discovered that my clothes and phones were in there minus Jenny's old jacket that I'd tossed on. If it had indeed been her jacket. I quickly changed and tucked my gown into the box and stuck it back where it had been. Silly in hindsight and perhaps a bit OCD. I tried turning on my phones. My personal one had a dead battery. The emergency one lit up but showed no bars. If I could get high enough, I'd be able to place a call.

I began the climb up the stairs. After the first flight I had to stop and sit. I was exhausted and shaky. I must have suffered more trauma than I'd realized. All I could do was one flight at a time then stop for a break. Slowly I got closer to the top. It seemed like all night had passed but according to the phone it had only been an hour since I started my climb up the stairs. The door at the top of the stairs had a piece of glass in it as well. I could see a light and walls through it. I slowly approached trying not to be seen as I did so. Again, empty of people. As I opened the door and stepped out into the security light, I could feel the cold air of the outdoors. There was a door right in front of me and I didn't hesitate to open it. This revealed the side yard of Jenny's house. As I looked around a bit confused, I could see that the back of the woodshed was the door I'd come through. I hadn't even known it was there. I was still out in the middle of nowhere but now I had the advantage of having a phone with bars. I hoped.

Pulling the phone from my pocket I could see a single bar on it. Then I shifted my feet slightly and the bar disappeared. I needed to head towards the edge of the property. Closer to town and the cell tower they'd placed there. This was a little more disorienting as all the snow had melted while I was being held. The area around me was very dark and I didn't want to use the flashlight on the phone as I didn't want the battery to die or for Sean and Frank to see it from a window. I moved quickly towards a section of driveway that was shrouded in darkness. Here I could see two vehicles parked near the house. One was the one Frank used to bring me to the house. The other must belong to Sean. No point trying to break in and hot wire one of them. My knowledge of cars goes more towards calling my father and asking what it means when there's a swish swish sound when I start it up. It's not that I couldn't do things – I knew how to change a tire and what the various lights meant – I just didn't always know what to do, I wasn't a mechanic or overly interested in cars outside of getting from point A to point B.

I turned and began to walk slowly along the side of the driveway. I didn't want to wear myself out before the night was over. I should be able to walk to town and, hopefully, get there before daybreak. If I didn't collapse. The tattoo on my palm still stung with a reminder of patience. I could hear myself breathing. Every now and then there'd be a snap, or a crack of a branch and I'd freeze. Looking around there was always a good reason. The wind would be picking up or a fox wandered out at the edge of the trees.

The tension was starting to get to me. At least the constant adrenaline was keeping me moving and not feeling the bruises and scrapes I'd suffered getting out of there. From a distance down the driveway, I glanced back and could see the security light. The house was still. A little further on and the drive curved so I wouldn't be able to see the house anymore. Once that happened, I'd be close enough to the road and tower to have signal.

The curve seemed to take forever. I pulled my phone out and found it now had two bars. I immediately dialed 911. It rang before giving me the automated menu asking if I was in need of police, ambulance, or fire. I was still shaking badly so hitting the right key was difficult. Once it routed, I felt relief.

"911 what's your emergency?"

"I've been kidnapped and held against my will for several days. I just managed to escape, and I need to get help now."

"Ok – do you know where you are? Can you see a street or address?"

"Yes it's 98253 Appleseed Dr. in the village of Toffcan."

"Are you able to get further away from the location?"

"Yes I can keep walking but the cell

service out here is bad, and I may lose signal if I move."

"Ok, start walking towards town. Stay on the line with me as long as possible while you walk. I'm dispatching a car to your location. Can you tell me what happened to you?"

I began telling her everything, starting with who was responsible. I didn't want the call to drop without her knowing that these were the men that held me. Then I told her about the door at the back of the woodshed. How the stairs went down for a long time. It was then that I heard a noise behind me that caused my stomach to fall. It was the sound of shouting coming from the direction of the house. While I'd been on the phone the sky had begun to lighten up. Sunrise. I hadn't even gotten down the street. Sean must have discovered that I'd fled. They were coming for me. I told the dispatcher, but the line had cut off.

I began to run. As I did, I started looking for a place where I could conceal myself. I Couldn't trust the neighbors. In villages like this everyone knew everyone else. I was more likely to get handed back to Frank or Sean if a local found me. At least the police were, usually, good people. They didn't want to arrest one of their own but at the same time they did enforce the law when things had gotten out of hand. I could hear a car coming up from behind me. Just ahead was a spot with heavy bushes next to some fencing. Most people wouldn't fit there but given how tiny I am I could make it work. I had to.

As I curled myself into a ball in the

sticker bushes, I could feel the wet ground start to soak through my clothes. It was the first time in my life that I felt thankful for being 4 foot 5. Unlike someone who was taller I'd be able to hide here without being seen. I just needed to stay still long enough and hope that no one saw me make the dive into the bushes in the first place.

The car went past very slowly as if it was following a trail. I held my breath hoping that whoever it was couldn't hear me. All I could hear was the pounding of my heart. It was the longest few seconds of my life. The car drove on. I waited for a minute before slowly uncurling and bringing my head up above the bush enough to see. Sean's car was down the road far enough that he wouldn't be able to tell I'd popped my head up but I still couldn't get out of the bush yet or he might see me. All I could do was wait. My palm had stopped hurting but it was itchy. I slid back down into my hiding place and tried to get a better look at the new tattoo. I was right, the hourglass was fancy. The tiger was set to pounce but what I hadn't been able to see before because of poor lighting was the white rabbit hopping over the top of the hourglass.

I began to have flashes of Alice in Wonderland. The white rabbit leading Alice down the rabbit hole while he frets about being late. I began to worry that Sean had continued down the road and I'd missed my chance to get away. Carefully I began to raise my head out of my hiding place again. There he was around the same place I'd seen him last but this time coming towards me. I dropped back down and stayed still. The car flew past me, and I could hear the shouting coming from inside. He must have opened a window. The words were indistinct, but I could tell that Sean was furious over not being able to find me. I heard the car slow and turn into the driveway. I took the chance and stood up. I began walking towards town again, keeping to the side of the road and watching for places I could hide should another car come my way. I had no service on my phone so I kept watch to see if I could find a signal. No sign of a police car either. I just kept moving. I walked past the end of the fence and into what looked like nothing but woods. Every mile or two there'd be a driveway. I had to hide in the woods three more times to avoid being seen by Sean. Not once did Frank come my way. It made me wonder if he'd wanted me to get out. To find a way to free myself. Perhaps he thought Sean had gone too far as well. The target on my arm began to burn. As I glanced down at it an arrow appeared in the center.

It felt the like all the blood rushed out of my head. I looked up the road just in time to see a police car rolling towards me slowly. They had their windows open and were looking at either side of the road. I stepped into the road and began to run towards them with my arms above my head waving to get their attention. The car was marked sheriff. They spotted me and pulled up as close as they could. A man I could only describe as every single stereotype of a small-town sheriff got out from behind the wheel. On the other side a tall dark woman with the most beautiful hair I'd ever seen stepped out a bright deputy badge on her chest. Her hand hovered on her gun. I couldn't blame her for that.

"My name is Dawn – I called 911. I was kidnapped. Can I please get in the car? I'm feeling cold and I'm in pain."

"Sure thing ma'am – first I need to ask if you have any weapons on you? Anything that's gonna stick one of us when we give you a quick pat down?"

"No Sir, I don't have any weapons on me or anything sharp, just my cell phones, one is dead in my left pocket and the one that's working in my right pocket." I submitted to the deputy patting me down before she opened the back passenger door and let me in. I began to feel the exhaustion of not sleeping and the adrenaline wearing off. I knew I needed to tell them everything before I passed out.

"Look ma'am we'll take your statement down at the station. It's a bit of a drive. I recommend getting some rest." The sheriff glanced at me in the rear-view mirror before pulling a U turn in the middle of the road and heading back in the direction of town. I laid my head against the window and closed my eyes.

4

A BREAK

A hand shaking my shoulder woke me. We'd arrived in front of the building – I could see movement in the restaurant. They must be getting ready to open for breakfast. There were only a couple of other cars parked on the block. I was shown into a set of offices that were small with an old-fashioned open jail at the back. The cells had a small half wall type partition in them where I assumed the toilet for each one would be. To one side was an office labelled sheriff and then a couple of desks in the middle of the room, none of them currently occupied. A set of counters was at the front where an elderly lady was sitting, a cup of coffee in one hand and an old-fashioned "paper" newspaper in the other. "Oh! My word!" the woman looked up and made eye contact with me. She suddenly started shuffling the paper back to the front page then began looking at it then at me.

"What is it, Mable?" the deputy looked like she'd already run out of patience with the woman. I suspect that she tended to speak at people regardless of if they were trying to work or not.

"The lady you have there, she's all

over the front page of the paper!" She turned the pages towards us, and it showed an image of me with the word missing in large bold letters across the top. From the quick scan I was able to get it said that I had simply disappeared and speculated on whether or not I had been lying about what had happened to me when it came to the trial.

"Huh, looks like we're going to be making a few phone calls. Mable, get the name of the lawyers that are looking for this young lady and bring them to me. Deputy, find out which departments are assigned to find her and call them. We need to get this sorted out. Well miss, you follow me, and I'll take your statement."

We went into the little office, and he got a glass of water for me from a jug in the corner. First, he made me tell him everything that happened, then we spent the next hour going over every detail. I could hear people outside the office coming and going. Phones ringing and hanging up. Turns out the sheriff's name was Bernard Albatross. He appeared to believe everything I said.

"Alright. Let's take a break. You must be hungry. I'm going to go over to the restaurant and get us something to eat. There's a little couch on the other side of the outer room – it's open so the deputy can keep an eye on you but at least you can get some rest." Bernard showed me out of the office and to where the couch was. After asking me what I wanted he ambled off to a door that linked to the main hall of the building. The Deputy looked over at me occasionally as if making sure I hadn't run off. Mable wandered over after a few minutes to chat with me.

"Do you need anything honey? If you like I can give you the newspaper to read over. I know that you can't tell me what happened to you, but I hope you know that we're here to help you and keep you safe." Close up Mable looked like a very sweet old woman. The kind of person that reminded me of my grandmother before she passed away. She also had a glint in her eye that said she had a wicked sense of humor.

"Thank you but the Sheriff is getting me some food. I would like to see the paper though. I don't even know what day it is." Mable brought over her newspaper and left me to read it alone. Ten days. It had only been ten days since I had been mobbed at the grocery store. There had been no real way to tell the days passing other than the clock and meals presented to me. Even then I hadn't been entirely sure that what Sean had said was accurate about me being in a coma for five days. Not a long period of time to have been held but plenty long enough for me. As I read the article, I could see comments from Jim telling the same story that I had told. Going to the house to hide from paparazzi only to disappear and no contact. Jim said that he'd gone out to the house with Frank and tried to find me but there had been no trace of me. All my things were still at the house so Jim had packed them up and brought them home. He'd notified the police and he was personally looking for me. Jim really was the best friend I could have. There was a notice in the paper as well advertising a reward in exchange for any information that led to me. I sat the newspaper to one side and started to rub my new tattoo. The itch was driving me crazy. I looked up towards the front door when a bell went off. There, standing in the middle of the front entry was Sean. I started curling up into a ball on the couch. I tried to make myself small so that he wouldn't see me. My heart started to pound hard, and my breathing cut to short gasps.

"Are you ok?" The deputy was leaning over me and touched my shoulder. Concern was written all over her face.

"He's one of the men that kidnapped me. His name is Dr. Sean Robbins. He did all kinds of tests and ran me through all kinds of machines. Ten days, the first five in a medically induced coma because he hit me in the back of the head. His husband is Frank Brogan. He's a journalist. I don't want him to see me."

"I'm sorry, we called the local doctor to have a look at you and he was the one on call. Follow me back to the office and I'll take care of it. Don't you worry." The deputy used her body to block me from being seen while we walked across the room. Once in the office she reached out and closed the blinds so that I couldn't be seen by anyone in the outer office.

After she closed the door, I couldn't see or hear anything. The door opened again and the Sheriff came in carrying a bag filled with to-go containers. He sat them on the desk and after signaling that I should find my order left me alone in the office again. I dug through and found my grilled cheese with fries. I refilled my water and started to slowly pick at the food. The thought of eating made me feel sick, but I knew I would need the energy for what was to come.

* * * * *

It was hours before the sheriff came back in. By then I'd finished my lunch and the smell of cold food from the other containers was beginning to bother me. Bernard sat down and began to dig through the bag. Slowly he brought out his container of food and, with a sigh, started picking at it.

"This is where we are at right now. We have people from a couple of police departments in the city on their way here. They have an open missing person's file on you, and you'll have to fill them in. Since this all started in their jurisdiction, they technically have the lead on the case. There are some people from the government that have contacted us and are on their way here as well. They want to know if this had anything to do with the court case you're supposed to be called for. The lawyers that are representing you are also coming since you're their client. At present, we have a Dr. Sean Robbins in our jail cell and we are looking for Mr. Frank Brogan. We sent people out to the house, and it looks like he's done a runner. We're preparing a B.O.L.O. for him. We've also called the gentleman that took out the missing persons on you. He's on his way – he said that he is bringing some of your things with him. I hope that's ok?"

"That'd be Jim – he's my business partner and long-time friend. He's got a spare key to my place; I hope he brings me some clean clothes."

"If you like you can go back out to the main room – Deputy Krebbs can show you where the washroom is. We have a shower available when your friend shows up."

"Thank you, Sheriff." I got up and walked out of the office. I settled myself on the couch. Looking around I could see Sean in the back jail cell. He was sitting quietly. There was a look of peace to his face. Like he thought that he would be let go soon.

I laid down on the couch and began to doze off. A deep sleep with all the noise of people coming and going and phones ringing wasn't possible, no matter how tired a person got. Jim was the first to arrive. His voice echoed as he stated his name at the front. I couldn't help jumping up and running in that direction. I didn't get far. Deputy Krebbs grabbed me and shook her head.

"You wait till we vet the people. Never just head towards them, ok? Safety first."

I nodded and waited for Jim to be cleared. The bag that he'd brought with him had to be searched and all his credentials verified against databases before they let him in the back. I couldn't wait any longer, I threw myself into his arms for a hug. He dropped the bag and picked me up off the floor and held me close. I couldn't help but cry.

"You can't tell me what happened yet. The police will need to verify it all. I spoke with Dutch and Andrews. They're heading up the hunt for Frank. They want me to call them once I've seen you to let them know you're still ok."

"I'm so glad you're here. Please tell me that you brought me clean clothes. I feel awful. I have a new tattoo on my palm and an arrow has added itself to my target. I need a little time to clean up and then I need some sleep. Sleep somewhere that I feel safe. Home would be best, but I'd like you to stay for the first night or two if its ok with you?"

"Of course. I can't even begin to describe how scared I was when you didn't answer either of the phones." Tears streamed down Jim's face as he spoke. If he was in this much of a state, then I can only imagine what my family was feeling.

"My sister? My parents?"

"I arranged for a special trip for them all together – a private yacht with no contact to avoid the news. That's what I was calling you about when you didn't answer all those days ago. I wanted you to know that they were safely away from all the issues for a while. Also, I was going to arrange for you to join them. You needed a break." Jim looked down at me and slowly lowered me to the floor.

"Yeah, I did. After all this I still need a break. Being strapped to a table for ten days was not exactly relaxing." I couldn't help but be a little angry with myself. I hadn't taken Jim's concerns into consideration – I'd been so traumatized in that moment that I'd just gone ahead and followed the first person to not flash a camera in my face. I owed Jim an apology for everything. I opened my mouth to tell him how sorry I was for everything I had put him through, for how wrong I'd been about Frank when the door to the front opened and two men in dark suits walked in. After providing their ID to Mable they were shown around the wall and to the office. Deputy Krebbs walked over to me with a frown on her face.

"Those will be the government guys that you have to speak with. The IDs were valid according to the computers. I don't know what department they were from – it's one that I don't recognize. Be careful." Krebbs cast a look at the office and gestured me to follow her to the office. Once inside I was offered a seat. The sheriff was standing in the back corner and the two agents occupied the only other chairs.

"We have a series of questions for you. Are you willing to answer them here or would you rather we went back to our office in town?" Agent One spoke – his pale blonde hair was cut close to his head. Blue eyes were now visible behind the glasses. Not a pleasant person by any means. Agent Two sat next to me in the other chair and remained silent. He had black hair cut in an identical way to his counterpart. Identical suit as well.

"I'd rather answer the questions here. My friend has shown up and before we begin, I'd like to have a shower and change into some clean clothes."

"That seems reasonable. We are going to close the restaurant and use it as our interview space. You go shower and the Deputy will bring you to us when you are done." Agent One made a dismissive gesture. I rose and left the room. Deputy Krebbs showed me to the showers in the locker room area that was off a little hall by the jail cell. Sean stared at me as I went past. It was disturbing.

Krebbs stood by the door and waited while I showered and dressed. It was the first time in days that I felt clean and human. I tucked my dirty clothes back into the bag. Digging through I didn't find anything else. I stepped out and for the first time since I met her Krebbs cracked a smile.

"Your hair looks like its standing on end. I've got a brush you can borrow. I also took the liberty of popping out during my lunch and picking you up a toothbrush. We keep some toothpaste in the counter caddy over there for when we have night shifts. You go ahead and finish up. Those government guys got food before they closed down the Watering Hole for the day."

"The Watering Hole?"

"Our local restaurant – some Australian guy married a girl from town years ago and opened it. Apparently, it was his favorite bar back home. They've handed it over to their kids now and moved to his hometown in Australia. Every Christmas the kids close the place down for a month and go see their parents."

"Thanks for the loan and the toothbrush. I'm feeling and smelling a hundred percent better."

"I know that I said this before, but those government guys give me the creeps – be careful when you're answering their questions. If you want to wait until your lawyers arrive, we can just hang out in here. They should be here in another hour or so. I can have Mable call and find out where they are."

"Thanks, but it's ok. I haven't done anything wrong and all I want is to get all the interviews over with so that I can go home and sleep for the next week. Jim is going to drive me and stay for a couple days. He sent my family on a special private cruise so that they wouldn't worry about me. They don't even know that I was kidnapped. He said he wanted me to go and spend some time with them relaxing away from all this mess."

"Wow. Is this Jim guy your boyfriend? He sounds like a keeper!"

"No – we've just known each other forever. His ex-wife was also a friend. Then she started sleeping with my now ex brother in-law and they tried to kill my sister, but I kept getting in their way, so they decided to kill me. They failed obviously. The problem is I had a skull tattoo come up. I was supposed to die. I didn't and the tattoo changed. So now on top of everything else I'm being dogged because of something I don't understand. My life is just a big mess."

"That's just a meeting of moments happening. You seem to be handling everything so far."

"Yeah sure – so I had a massive panic attack at the grocery store which led to walking away with a kidnapper. I thought I'd be safe. I should have taken some time off from work and taken a vacation."

"Sounds like that would have been a better choice. You've got to live with the decisions you make. It's how you handle the consequences that determines the kind of person you are. From my perspective you're at least a decent person if not an actual good person."

"Thanks – that makes me feel much better. Still, I need to go deal with the government guys. If I can just get through all these interviews, I'll let Jim send me off to whatever yacht he's tucked my family away on and stay there until I'm required to come back."

Krebbs led me from the locker room and with a wary look on her face took me out into the restaurant. There the Sheriff was standing next to the counter watching the government men. I was shown to a seat in the booth across from them. The table had been cleared and a glass of water was waiting for me. Agent One got up once I was seated and showed both the Deputy and the Sheriff out of the room. As he seated himself again, he began the conversation.

"Take us through what happened starting from the very beginning."

"Well, I was at the grocery store

and…"

"No; you've mistaken me. We want to know what happened from the time just before your skull tattoo appeared until this moment now." Agent One stared at me like I was a criminal. I began to regret not letting the Deputy talk me in to waiting for my lawyers.

"It's a very long story." I could only hope that making this statement would cause the Agents to let me give them the abridged version.

"Please begin." Agent One pulled out a recording device and started it. I had no choice but to begin at the beginning of this mess.

*   *   *   *   *

The sun had set by the time I finished. I hadn't been allowed a stop for more than a little bit of water from my cup. Once done I was sure that the kidnapping had nothing to do with the existing trial. These agents must see the same. I had done nothing to cause this. They retired a few feet away and Agent One pulled out a cell phone. Agent Two kept an eye on me to make sure I didn't try to leave.

"Yes Sir. Of course, sir. Right now, sir." Agent One hung up the phone and whispered something to Agent Two who nodded in agreement. Agent Two went out the front of the restaurant to their nondescript black SUV that everyone knew belonged to the government. Agent One came back over but remained standing.

"If you'd like to use the washroom or

would like something to eat now is the time." As I got up to head to the washroom Agent One followed me. He even followed me in and checked the bathroom to make sure the window was too small for anyone to get in. It was a little odd, but I assumed it was for my own protection.

When I came out of the washroom, I walked past Agent One. Suddenly everything went dark, and I was restrained from behind. A hand went over my mouth pressing fabric against my face. I felt myself lifted off the ground and could hear someone telling me not to struggle. Why do I keep trusting the wrong people?

5

THE GOVERNMENT

I was buckled into a car. I tried to scream but I was having trouble just breathing with all the fabric across my mouth. My wrists and ankles were bound. This was beginning to feel more and more familiar. An odd sense of calm came over me. There could only be one thing that had happened. The agents black bagged me.

I'd watched shows with Jim where the government had done this to people. I hadn't believed that this was how it happened. There was no reason for me to be scared. Normally this only happened to terrorists. Why on earth would they do this to a tiny woman who'd committed no crimes?

"Once we arrive at our destination you will be allowed to see again. You will be kept safe. You needn't worry about that." The unfamiliar voice must belong to Agent Two. I tried to subtly stretch the restraints. "If you continue to do that, I will be forced to knock you out until our arrival."

There was nothing left to do but allow them to take me where they would. So, I took a nap. Hours must have passed, and I woke when we hit a bumpy road. We'd slowed and I could smell the ocean. If we had made it that far we'd been on the road for at least six hours. We stopped and I was pulled out of the car. The bag was removed from my head, and I could see that the sun was just starting to rise. We were in a heavy industrial area of a harbor. I could see what looked like an abandoned building to one side. Windows were broken, random pieces of metal were strewn around the lot. The parking lot itself had heaved in several locations and the cement was all broken up. We slowly made our way over to a door in the side of the building. Since my ankles were restrained, I couldn't take big steps. They lifted me over the door sill so that I wouldn't trip. Inside the building it was just as much of a mess. It looked like squatters had been cleared out recently. There was a bank of elevators in the center that looked like they hadn't been used in over a decade.

A tightness settled into my stomach as I was escorted into the elevator. Agent Two hit a button for the lower parking garage. There was a jump up and down as the elevator began to move. I could only assume this was leading to what was generally called a black site.

When the doors opened, I could see a set of desks and computers all spread out. There were different kinds of thick wire groups running all over the place. A set of offices had been built on the right of the elevators and at the far end of the room some type of cell had been set up. I was led over to the cell and placed inside.

Once there the restraints were removed, and I stretched and moved around. It was a fair-sized space. A single bed was along one wall, and a partial partition was in front of the toilet. Next to that was a full-sized cubby that would allow for some privacy when showering in it. Agent One walked away as I explored my new surroundings. Agent Two stood there and watched me like he was trying to decide if I was going to cause them any issues.

"This is just temporary. Our boss has some questions for you. Then he will decide if you will be detained further." I was right – it had been Agent Two telling me not to fight.

I would go through with the interview. Did I have a choice? It couldn't be any worse than some of the interviews I'd already had. If they thought that they were going to keep me here or anywhere without my permission, they had another think coming. I began looking for ways to free myself from the cell just in case they decided I would need to be detained further. The mattress itself was made from some kind of indestructible material, but I did manage to accidentally rip the sheet when it snagged on a piece of sharp metal that was sticking down under the frame of the bed. Typical government – cut corners and get the cheapest contract to make the things they needed. At least if I worked on that piece of metal, I may be able to get it out and have a weapon on hand. I'd have to be careful though, with my past they were likely watching to see if I would make a run for it.

Eventually Agent Two walked away and joined Agent One across the room at a set of computers. I pretended to lay there asleep while I was observing what everyone was doing. When you watch people long enough, you'll see that they tend to make the same motions over and over. Sit at a computer and type for a while. Get up and head to what is likely a washroom on one side of the elevators. Sit back down and type some more. Confer with someone else at the same computer bank. Go get coffee, go back, sit down, work. Over and over again. The only time the routine seemed to change was when a short bald man in a dark suit came in. Then several people followed him into an office on the other side of the elevator. Agents One and Two went to wait outside the door. After a short time, they were called in. I could see them speaking when suddenly the man who'd had a seat behind the desk slammed his hand down and then started to speak and gesture angrily. Shortly after Agents One and Two left the room and made their way over to my cell.

"You'll be coming with us so please stand up and face the wall." Agent One was doing all the talking again. I complied and they placed restraints on me. I was led into the office and helped into a chair across from the man. Everyone that had been in there left. We were alone.

"I've had a word with my agents. It seems that they stepped outside of their job description by asking you questions that are above their pay grade. I'm sorry for that. Also for those restraints. I won't have them removed since they are for my safety."

His voice had an odd raspy quality to it, as if he'd spent years smoking before quitting.

"All I want is to go home sir. I haven't done anything wrong."

"That's true you haven't done anything wrong, however, you are different. We have gone through and found all the information that a Dr. Robbins had gathered on you. We have access to some equipment that he doesn't, and we'd like your permission to run you through it."

"Does permission really matter at this point? If I were to say no you'd just go ahead and do it anyways but probably you wouldn't be nearly as gentle with me."

His mouth quirked into a sarcastic smile as he thought about the situation.

With a gesture to the agents on the other side of the door he continued, "Ms. Hobbes has agreed to let us do the testing. Be gentle with her. Once the tests have been run, we can set her up with a safe house until it's her time to go to the trial."

I was escorted out of the office and down a nearly hidden hallway. There were plexiglass windows lining both sides. Some of the rooms had cages with mice or rats in them. Others showed that there was some kind of air conditioning keeping the room icy cold. All of them had people coming and going. At the end of the hall, I was shown into a room that held some odd look machines. I didn't recognize any of them. A man in a lab coat with a clipboard stood there with a smaller woman that was dressed similarly. I was set on to a table and the agents stepped out of the room.

"Hi there, my name is Dr. Bradley, and this is my associate Dr. Kate. We're going to start by taking some blood samples. Then there will be a couple of scans and after that we should be all done." His voice was a pleasant one to listen to. He still had most of his hair although it had begun to thin on top and was a stark white color. Dr. Kate had her bright orange hair pulled back in a thick braid that fell down her shoulder. Wisps were escaping near her temples. A thick set of glasses perched on her nose.

She pulled over a little stainless-steel trolley with a bunch of plastic tubes and bags. Grasping my arm, she rolled up the sleeve and began the process of drawing blood. After several vials had been taken, I needed to lay down. They were kind enough to give me some juice, but my stomach was beginning to feel very empty. I hadn't eaten since lunch the day before. Dr. Kate smiled at me as she put the vials into a cooler.

"You look a little pale. Do you need some more juice?"

"I need a meal – I haven't eaten since yesterday at lunch. Even then it wasn't much. How long will the scans take?"

"About an hour. You can't have food before them, but you can have as much juice as it takes to help. I'll arrange for a couple of meals for you as soon as we're done here." She seemed genuinely concerned. I was rolled over to the first scanner. It looked like the same kind of MRI machine that Sean had put me in. Once I was laid on the bed my restraints were removed.

"You'll need to stay completely still for this. Can you do that for us?" Bradley seemed happy with how things were going. I did my best to stay completely still. The machine ran a couple of times. "We've gotten an overview of your brain and a couple of close ups of the structure that Robbins noted in his file."

"One more scan and then we can get you back to your cell. I spoke with the agents outside the door, and they've arranged some food for you when we're done here." Kate gave me a soft almost motherly smile.

"May I ask a question? Do you think they will let me go home alive when all this is over?" Kate and Bradley exchanged a look and didn't make eye contact with me. I was helped to stand and then asked to strip down so that they could scan all the tattoos I had. It was uncomfortable to stand in the machine and have a bright light spin around my body. I began to feel lightheaded and weak. Suddenly the machine went dark, and a hand reached out and took my arm. I was led out and my clothes were pushed into my hands. I dressed in muted lighting and by the time I was finished the area had lit up normally once more.

The restraints were put back on and I was taken back to my cell. I could smell food and there was a little table now set up in the cell. A tray of food was set on it. Chicken tenders and fries with what looked like Sprite in a cup next to it. At least it was something recognizable. I ate and then pushed the table next to the door. Then I laid down and waited. Slowly the room started to empty out. First all the various people working on experiments left. Then the offices cleared. People from the main room began to finish things up and leave. Soon there was just Agent Two and a janitor.

Agent Two pulled a chair up next to the cell watching to make sure I didn't try to speak with the janitor as he cleared garbage cans and washed the floor. There was a sense of relief when the janitor was on the far side of the room and double checking to make sure he had everything before he left. Agent Two turned ever so slightly towards me.

"There're cameras everywhere around this place. As long as I'm careful I can talk and no one will know what I'm saying, the fools didn't put in cameras that have audio available on them. Okay, first this is not a government group. I was pulled from a standard security team and told to not speak to you unless I had to. There are a couple guys here that I think are legit military but other than that it's some kind of private facility that wants to use you to find a cure for the tattoos. They aren't going to let you live. Just like that other guy wanted to do, once they hit a dead end, they'll kill you to get the information they want. FYI, I know Jim. I worked for the firm that he hired when you got your skull. I was part of the whole trap thing you did." I rolled to my side to face the wall so that I could speak without being seen.

"Help me get out of here then. All I

need is a small window to work with and I can escape. We can even make it look like you were taken by surprise."

"I don't care if they know that I did it. I'm done with this job at the end of tomorrow anyways. It was supposed to be done at the end of today, but they asked me to stay on as overnight guard. I can arrange for a power outage to the building then I can let you go, and no one will be the wiser. There's only one issue: no stairs. For the elevator to work there must be power. The camera in the elevator will see us. You'll have to take me as a hostage."

"Not a problem. Is the gun your carrying real?"

"Yeah."

"Ok, contact Jim. Explain what

happened. Give him the address and have him pull up with cops, it's not like the elevator has a code or anything. Just give Jim the floor button that needs to be pushed. They can come down and find me. Then this whole place can be shut down."

"I would have to wait till tomorrow when I'm officially not on the job anymore. If I do it today then I could lose my job. The NDA didn't extend after I was done. Silly really given how easy it is to find my way back here."

"No – that's a bad sign. It means that once they've gotten rid of all the temp hires like you that they'll move me somewhere no one will ever find me again."

"There's at least two more people that

they have to clear first. I had a beer with one of them last night while we were waiting for orders. He's not due to be finished his contract till the night after tomorrow. They won't be able to move you till then."

"Ok. Fine. In the morning. Literally as soon as you walk out that door. Watch your back – I wouldn't be surprised if they tried to put a bullet in it." Agent Two went back to his desk and I went to sleep. I could only hope that tomorrow would bring me some kind of help. Maybe with a little luck I would be out of here and off to a yacht with my family. Or at the very least off home for a shower and more than one meal a day.

6

ESCAPE

I decided I needed a shower when I woke in the morning. The water was icy cold. Agent Two was still here but made an effort to not look in my direction while I got clean. As I sat running my fingers through my hair over and over again in the hopes that it wouldn't become too knotted, people began to arrive for their shifts. Some new faces appeared as well. Several men that looked like they were either military or mercenaries. When the doctors arrived Agent Two was taken aside and spoken with. He was then led by the military looking men to the elevators. I could only hope that he would come out of this alive and do what I needed.

My stomach began to ache. No food was being prepared or brought to me. I should have known that I wouldn't get fed by these people. As I sat waiting for the doctors to arrange for more tests a red light went off and everyone froze in place looking around them. Then doctors began to pour out of the lab hallway. They were all talking and yelling. I couldn't make out what they were saying as an alarm had begun to sound very loudly next to my cell.

The boss came out of his office and

began to issue orders. The medical people went back down the halls and came back with various sized cases while the people around the office began to take apart their equipment and load it all into crates that had apparently been serving as desks. I took the opportunity to hide in the shower area. From a crack in the cubical I could see people loading the elevator and leaving. The military men that had escorted Agent Two out came back down and immediately went into the office. I could see the boss arguing with them about something. When one of them gestured towards my cell I knew that I didn't have long until they decided I was a loose end that needed removal.

There was a banging by the elevator that caught my attention. The doors opened and a swat team pushed their way into the room. It was chaos. People were running and trying to find places to hide. Shots were being fired at those holding weapons. All I could do was try to make myself as small as possible and try not to be caught in crossfire. I heard doors banging open from the offices, but it was too risky to sneak a look and see what was happening. It seemed to go on forever before the sounds slowly quieted. The only sound left was the alarm.

"Someone kill that alarm – it's starting to give me a headache!" The voice sounded familiar. "Hey Dawn, where are you? It's ok to come out now."

Slowly I rose in my hiding place and came around the partitions. Not enough that I would be immediately seen but enough to see out. There were people all over the ground, some had obviously been shot, others were in restraints. Swat uniforms were everywhere. A flashlight danced across my face causing me momentary blindness so I was unable to see what was going on. I stepped carefully from my hiding place and raised my hands up so there could be no mistaking me as a target.

"You're still alive? You know you've done enough to impress me now, right?" The last was said with a laugh to it and I recognized the voice of Andrews - one of my favorite detectives.

"Ah come on Andrews, it sounds like you're easy to impress!" I couldn't help laughing giddily as I stepped closer to the doors. "Are you going to let me out of here? I'm starving!"

The swat officers that were with Andrews and Dutch kept looking back and forth between us like we were all crazy. Dutch fumbled around and found the keys to the cell. I was escorted over to the elevators and loaded in for the ride up. Again, the elevator did a little jump before it began its ascent. I was looking forward to seeing some daylight.

"Jim filled us in on what happened. When you disappeared with those men from the restaurant the Sheriff and the Deputy were both mad as hornets. They're both insisting on coming in to see you once we have you safely tucked away. Honestly, I'll be glad to meet them face to face, they seem like good people. Oh, and there's been a development: we found and arrested Frank Brogan." Dutch kept a constant conversation going as we rose. I think that he was as uncomfortable with the elevator as I was.

When the doors finally opened, I was shown to the outside. It must have been close to noon with how bright the sun was. I was tucked into a marked police car and driven to the station. There I was shown to an interview room and Andrews settled himself across the table from me. Dutch got a little smile on his face as he stepped out of the room.

"Dutch is going to get you some food since you always seem to be starving. He should be back soon. Jim is waiting at my desk in the bullpen. I hate to do this first but it's better to get your statement while it's still fresh in your mind." Andrews started the recording device and stated the date and time, then he asked for information to confirm who I was. I began making my statement and after about a half an hour Dutch came in with food and drink for me before settling down in the chair next to Andrews. I continued to explain what had happened while inhaling as much of the grilled cheese and fries as I could.

"You've really been through it haven't you Dawn?" Dutch couldn't help shaking his head over the latest situation. A knock on the door was followed by a man shoving his way into the room. My lawyer, looking like he was going to roast someone over an open fire if he didn't get his way, had arrived.

"My client has done nothing wrong and is being pursued over a silly tattoo. And what do you do? You dump her into an interrogation room, denying her the right to representation and interview her without permission! I'll sue this whole department!" Mr. Allers was a small man with a big booming voice that could silence an entire court room when he wanted to. He was dressed in a high-end suit, soft grey in colour that matched his hair. His glasses were sliding off his nose and his face had gone bright red with his speech.

"Mr. Allers. So glad you could finally join us. Your client was just giving us her statement. The reason we are using the interrogation room was for several reasons. First and foremost is that this recording device is the only one working in the entire department at the moment. Second there's a table. Ms. Hobbes stated upon rescue that she was starving. This way she doesn't have to sit with the food in her lap. Lastly this location is in the middle of a department filled with other detectives who will do everything in their power to protect her from the people who kidnapped her. Please have a seat and feel free to listen to the remainder of this interview." It was clear that Andrews had little liking for Allers. They had probably banged heads in a court room at some point. I finished describing what had happened that morning up to the point where the swat team had come in.

"At this point we'd like to offer you police protection. You'd be allowed to go home and gather some things then we'd take you to a safe house where you'd stay until the trial is over. After that sadly you would be on your own again, however, knowing your business partner I'm sure that hiring some extra security isn't going to break the bank either." Dutch was grinning over the look on Allers face when a safe house was brought up. It looked like he'd swallowed a lemon.

"I'd like to speak with my client alone please." Allers waited until the room was cleared before checking that the recording machine was off. "You should be in a safe house, but the one I have set up. Police safe houses are not the best, there's a list that anyone from the department can access which includes if it's actively in use. It'd be nothing for someone to find you."

"I agree that a safe house with the police is not a good idea. That being said, I don't want to go to the one you have set up either. I need to take some cash out and do this myself. I need to completely fall off the map. Do we know who it was that kept me in that facility?"

"A pharmaceutical company, they've been researching the tattoos. They hired a bunch of mercenaries to grab you. From what I've been able to find out they own that building and from the experiments that have been recovered it's obvious that they have gone outside the Geneva convention by using humans as guinea pigs. If the whole company isn't shut down, then a large portion of it will lose their licensing. But back to the relevant topic. The safe house I've set up is completely off the map. No one will find you there."

"I need to think about it. I'm still hungry. Can you send Jim in here and maybe go pick out some chips or something from the vending machine?"

"Alright. We aren't done discussing this though." Allers stepped out of the room and a minute later Jim came in. He pulled me in to a hug.

"You've got to stop doing this. Quit disappearing on me. I don't think I can take much more."

"Neither can I. Look Jim, the cops want to put me in one of their safe houses and Allers wants me in the one he has set up. All I want is to see my family and if that isn't possible then I want to go home. I want to sit and watch movies and eat. Is there anything we can do to set that up?"

"I'll speak with Andrews and Dutch. Allers is your problem though. He won't listen to me. I've tried several times to tell him that you wouldn't go for a safe house, and he set one up anyway."

"Ok. Go on and when Allers comes back in I'll tell him no. He can't force me to comply." A shiver ran down my back as I had a flash of being told to comply by Robbins and Agent Two. "Also, you remember that security company you hired for me last year. Well, there was a guy that was on contract to the pharmaceutical company that grabbed me. He said that he was going to call you and help me escape. We need to make sure he doesn't lose his job over this."

"I'll make a call and find out but I didn't get any calls from anyone. I was here when Dutch and Andrews got a call that caused all Hell to break loose.

Suddenly they were out the door and had a full squad with them."

"Maybe he called them directly. I'll ask." I felt puzzled by the fact that Agent Two hadn't called Jim. It would have been another layer to keep him safe from being exposed. Allers stepped back in as soon as Jim walked out.

"Look Mr. Allers, I'm not going to your safe house. Jim is looking into me having police protection at home and failing that he and I will set up a place for me that's safe. I know it's not what you want to hear but my decision is final."

"Alright Ms. Hobbes. I can't force you to see reason. Remember this moment when something happens and feel free to call and apologize when you do."

With a derisive sniff Allers walked out of the room. I tried to remember that the reason I had picked him was due to how many cases he had won in trial situations.

Andrews and Dutch came back in the room with Jim following close behind. It was obvious that they were having a disagreement. This didn't stop until we were all seated at the table again.

"Look Dawn we would prefer the safe house, but I get it that you don't want to be taken to yet another location that you don't know with people you have no reason to trust. There's only so much we can do for you at home. We can post people outside the house and rotate them just like we did last year. That's about all we can do though, and you remember what happened."
Andrews threw a glance at Dutch who

had ended up in a hospital bed during that patrol.

"I know Andrews. I just can't face another location right now. Jim can bring me groceries, so I don't have to go out. I can work from home. I will do everything I can to minimize the chances of something going wrong."

"If that's what you want then we will get someone over to your house and set up a rotation." He and Dutch both seemed worried that the police presence wasn't going to be enough to keep me safe in my own home. I was a bit worried myself but more than anything I just wanted to go home.

* * * * *

The Target

Jim drove me to my house as soon as we had permission to leave. I went through my cupboards and fridge. Everything stank. We cleared out all the garbage and then I went to run a bath. I couldn't face the idea of cooking. Jim waited until he was sure I was in the bath before leaving to pick up groceries. I spent hours washing and then draining the tub just to fill it again and soak more dirt and smell off my body.

When I finally got out and found some comfy clothes, I put a load into the washing machine. I wandered over to the tv and turned it on. It was set to a news channel. My re-emergence was the top story. There was a great deal of speculation as to where I had been and why I had disappeared. I tried flipping through channels but there was always some kind of commercial or banner at the bottom of the screen talking about what was coming up tonight and my name was across everything. I turned the tv off. I couldn't take the silence though. I had plugged my phone in when I got home. There must be enough power now to turn it on and let me listen to music.

There were a ton of messages on it. Most of them from Jim. I cleared the notifications and ignored them for now. Music was the important part at the moment. I selected my favorite Fleetwood Mac album and turned on the Bluetooth speaker that was on the island. I couldn't believe how much I had missed music. I felt like weeping over how good it felt to not be bombarded by people and news. To not feel fear for the first time in months. I didn't want to move. It wasn't until the album was finished that I noticed how hungry I was. Jim still hadn't returned from the grocery store with food, so I picked up my phone and started filtering through the messages that I had received.

There were several from my family thanking me for having Jim arrange the vacation, pictures of Little Whale swimming with Lynn for the first time and my parents sitting on the deck with drinks in hand. Some messages with increasing worry from Andy who had thanked me for recommending him for promotion. There were several texts from unknown numbers, many calling me cruel things because I had disappeared, some begging for interviews and a couple of them were men that wanted to "get to know" me better after seeing images of me on tv. Lastly, I looked at the ones from Jim. I skipped past the ones that I knew would just be his worry, followed by the notifications that he was coming to see me. The most recent message was that before heading to the grocery store, he had stopped at home to pick up some clothes so that he could stay with me for a few days.

I sent a message asking where he was. While I waited on a reply I went into my office and spotted my laptop bag sitting on the desk. Getting my computer set back up helped me feel less like my life had been turned on its head. My phone made a racket on the counter as a message came in. Jim texting back – he'd been waylaid by reporters at his house. Most of them had been rousted from my property by

the police when they set up the
protection detail. He was finished at
the store and was about to head back to
my place. All I could hope was that he
had the good sense to pick up enough
food for a couple weeks. I had
promised to limit my exposure so that
the job the police had would be easier.

Picking another album at random I
checked my laundry to see if it was
ready to be swapped. Another half
hour to go. I hadn't realized how much
work and tv had taken over my life. I
had nothing else to do around the
house. When I was young, I had
enjoyed so many different hobbies.
Once I met Annie and Jim things had
changed. I spent more time hanging
out with them, then opening the
business. My life had been consumed
by work and then I'd come home tired

The Target

and unable to do too much. It was time to make a change. I needed to cut back on the things that exhausted me and do more of the things I enjoy. Gardening was great but we have five to seven months of winter here. I could start making ornaments again, I loved to paint. Yes, I could do that. I remembered learning to knit when I was little, that seemed practical since I could learn to make nice sweaters for myself. Decision made – As soon as Jim returned, I would speak with him about spending less time at the office.

* * * * *

"Sorry it took so long; I know you must be hungry." Jim heaved another set of bags onto the counter. When he started bringing things in, I had begun unloading. There was enough food here for a month. He hadn't stopped talking since his return. I was given a full description of what had happened at his home and the store. All it did was reinforce my choice.

"We need to talk." Those words made Jim freeze in place. We'd had conversations like this back when I had dumped a boyfriend. Jim had helped me practice not hurting the guy's feelings.

"What's the topic?" he had slowed taking things out of bags. He was very careful as he sat a bottle of wine on the counter.

"Work. I think I need to step back for a while. When I return, I need to have some more balance in my life. While you were out I realized just how much time I spend on doing things for the company and when I'm done for a day I'm so exhausted that all I do is watch tv. I miss having hobbies and having time to enjoy them."

"Oh, that's no problem. Honestly, I was going to speak with you about that too. I want to bring in and train some more people. You disappearing like that caused me to feel the same way. I had nothing to keep me distracted while the police were doing their jobs and I couldn't concentrate on the company twenty-four-seven. If I felt that way, I figured you must be in worse shape. You've done the majority of the work on the company over the years not to mention balancing me and Annie's personalities when she was around." Jim looked relieved that I wanted a break from work. I would have to have a chat with him about us and our feelings but that was for another day. For now, I just wanted something to eat.

"I'm glad you understand. Hand me that cheese and I'll get started on a quick dinner." Fancy grilled cheese and chips it was.

7

HOMELESS

I slept like I was dead. Jim had lifted me upright and was shaking me trying to get me to wake up. All I wanted was a couple more minutes. I suddenly felt my stomach hit something hard and all the breath was knocked out of me. I began coughing. When I tried to get a breath, I began to choke. Opening my eyes all I could see was an odd red light and lots of smoke. My house was on fire!

Suddenly I was in the dark and cold outside. I realized I was barely dressed. The police had formed a group at the edge of the property and Jim had hauled me over his shoulder to get me out of the burning building. We collapsed to the ground next to the officers. I felt hands on my body lifting me off Jim. He was having a hard time getting air. Two ambulances were there, Jim had a mask put over his face and was loaded into one. I fought to try and get in with him. Breathing had become very difficult, and I sucked the oxygen as a mask was placed over my face. The police insisted I go in my own ambulance.

I caught glimpses of a fire truck and firemen working to contain the burning to just my home. I was losing everything. All I wanted was to be safe and happy. With everything I had gone through I could only assume that I had been targeted. My mind became overwhelmed, and things began to blank out. Then everything went dark.

When I woke out of my blackout, I was on a bed hooked up to a monitor. There was a mask over my face and an unfamiliar doctor in the room.

"Welcome back. Please don't touch the mask – your oxygen sats are still a little low. We'll be keeping you here for another day then the police will take you to their safe house. The gentleman who pulled you from the fire is taking a little longer to recover. We're going to keep him for a week. I believe the police said as soon as he was released, they would have him join you." The doctor was too chatty.

Everything seemed off kilter and odd. Had I been kidnapped again?

When he finished making some notes on a clipboard chart, he left the room. I could see policemen outside the door. It looked like a real hospital, but I couldn't trust anyone anymore. I was able to see out a window. It was late afternoon and a clear day for a change. I would wait until after the shift change to sneak away. I didn't care if I was paranoid, I didn't feel safe.

I rested off and on until it started to get dark. Periodically a nurse would check in on me, but she never spoke. The officers outside the door changed out. There were two of them at the moment, a nurse had left her desk and was flirting with one of them. The other one rolled his eyes and made an excuse to leave the door. It was now or never. I pulled all the cords off and hit the silencer on the alarm. I waited until the nurse turned her head away from my room and the cop had his back to me.

With a quick glance down the hall, I saw the big red, clearly marked, exit sign that must lead to a stairwell. I ran as quietly as I could and slipped through the door. Unfortunately, I was still in the standard gown that every medical facility issued. First, I'd need clothes and then some money. I needed to get out of here. On the wall at each level there was a list painted next to the door telling people what the floor contained. The administration floor had the lost and found along with the doctor's locker room. That would be my first stop. I slipped along the surprisingly empty floor. It looked like most people had left for the day and the shift change had already taken place. I was able to break the lock on the room labeled lost and found using a set of forceps I had found on a tray sitting in the hall. In there I dug through and found some sweatpants that I was able to tie around my waist then roll under for the length. A loose T-shirt and an old but clean jacket. I found some shoes, but they were far too big for me. I added several layers of mismatched socks to each of my feet before shoving them into the shoes. It wasn't fancy and I looked like I was a homeless teenager.

That was when it hit me. I was homeless. My house had burned down. The only place I could think of going now was Jim's house. I was sure that he'd let me stay there. The problem with that was the fact it was likely being staked out by tv crews. Lynn's place would lead any attackers I had to my family. With a deep breath decided that I would just have to figure it out when the moment came. I slipped back out of the door. The doctors' locker room was tempting. I could probably find money there. It would make life easier. As I began to take a couple steps towards it, I could hear some laughing coming from that direction. I bolted to the stairwell door again and decided to flee.

Thumping down the stairs I hoped that there was an exit door at the bottom, and I wouldn't have to detour through any other hallways. I nearly fell a few times because I couldn't feel anything through all the layers of socks and the odd feeling of the shoes being too heavy for me. Finally, I managed to get down to the bottom. There was only one door. It led to a hallway labelled Morgue. I began to shiver as I pushed the door open. It was very cold in the hallway. The darkness was only broken here and there by a security light or a light on an exit sign. I followed the signs hoping that everything here was closed for the night. If we were still in the same town I lived in, then it was unlikely that the morgue had a night shift. Not enough people. But the sooner I got out of here the less likely it would be that I would get caught.

Suddenly the path ended. Nothing but a heavy metal fire door between me and freedom. I stepped out and discovered I was on the side of the hospital. I walked as if I was simply passing through on my way somewhere else. Police cars and cameras were everywhere. I could see Andrews and Dutch speaking to them, saying that they couldn't comment on an open case and to please leave the hospital property or they'd be escorted away. I wanted to speak with them. I wanted to find out if Jim really was ok.

I turned and kept walking. For now, I needed to disappear. So long as everyone thought I was under police protection at the hospital no one would be looking for me. After putting some distance between me and the facility I slowed and began to wander a little. I knew that I could get into Jim's house. I could shower and borrow some clothes. There should be some food and cash there as well.

The walk took all night. My feet were

killing me. I didn't have any blisters from the shoes, but all the layers of socks made my feet sweat and itch. They also caused increasing pain in my feet, legs and hips. The sun was beginning to rise. I had heard and seen police cars driving around all night. Someone had to have discovered that I was missing by now.

None of them had looked twice at me when they drove past. When I was a block away from Jim's house I could see what was happening. There was a police car parked in the driveway and cameras on the sidewalk out front. I knew of a back way into his home though. It was the direction I had planned on taking. If you passed by the house at the end of the street there was a little gate. People usually assumed that it led to the person's back yard.

What it actually led to was a little alley path, overgrown with plants and carefully tended by everyone on the block. It wasn't locked, ever. I slipped down the alley and felt immensely better for not being out on the streets and very visible as the daylight began increasing. The path was heavily shaded and smelled of wet earth. For a moment I was able to feel peace.

A wrought iron gate with the initials J and A told me I had reached Jim's house. I remembered when they'd gotten the gate. Jim had gotten drunk and insulted Annie. To make amends he'd ordered a very expensive gate fully personalized from a favorite sculptor of Annie's taste. She'd forgiven him and weeks later insisted I help with the landscaping to make the new gate and yard more private. She'd sat in a folding lounge chair with a drink in her hand and complained the entire time about how she would have gotten something solid. I dug and planted lots of crawlers there so that it would create a privacy screen between the house and gate. It looked like neither Jim nor Annie had bothered much with taking care of the plants after that. They'd gotten very overgrown, and it felt like stepping through a portal into a fairy garden. The heads of red and white roses were falling over in giant bushes. Lilacs had grown as large as the small cherry trees I'd put in. All of this worked in my favor. No one could see me working my way up to the back door and it muffled any noises from the shoes.

I got to the covered patio which had

been kept clear of plants. Sitting down on a chair I began to peel off the shoes and socks. A little cool air helped them feel better. Turning to the door I glanced down at my hands to make sure my fingers were reasonably clean. Jim had gone to biometric locks not long after they'd come out. He'd used me to learn how to program people's prints into the software. I doubt he even remembered that he'd done it.

Placing my thumb on to the pad I heard the scanner spin up. A light scanned from the top to the bottom and back up again. The lock on the door flipped and the alarm went off as I stepped inside. I ran to the security pad next to the door and punched in my code. Annie had insisted I have my own access code to her house in case she didn't want to go and get something. I had spent as much time in this house as in my own over the years.

Jim had begun to redecorate after Annie went to prison. All the art – most of it I thought was ugly and weird – was gone. In its place there were some pictures framed of Jim's family and a few images of us from back in college. Half the walls had been painted in a soft grey blue tone. The rest were still the odd rose-pink colour that Annie had insisted on. All the gold gilt and heavy plaster pieces had been sanded off. I could see patch work in places where furniture had been moved and banged a hole in to walls. Other than the couch covered in a plastic sheet there was no other furniture in the living room. I didn't turn on any lights as I walked along the back of the house to the dining room. Once there I could turn to the left and between the dining room and kitchen were the back stairs. I slowly climbed the steps counting each one to make sure I didn't miss one and fall. All the doors at the top must have been closed. It was pitch black up there.

At the top I knew I could turn left for the guest room and right to the master suite. Jim had thought remodeling the upstairs to make the master as large as it was had been a silly idea. Annie had fought hard and won the style that she wanted. I opened the door and the light from the street came in and let me see the room. The bed and frame had been replaced already. A comfortable looking leather recliner had been added along with a tv on the wall across from the bed. To my left was the door to the closet and beyond that the door for the master bathroom. I turned into the first door and closed it behind me. Since the closet had no windows, I could turn the light on and see what was there.

Most of the closet was empty. Annie had been big on collecting designer items. Jim had his suits on one side and behind them were some T-shirts and a bank of drawers. I went over and began to dig through looking for some clean clothes. In the bottom drawer I found something completely unexpected. An entire set of my own clothes. Things that I'd forgotten existed. I'd come over to hang out with Jim one weekend and forgotten the clothes when I left. I must have left them in the guest bath when I'd changed. It was a relief. I pulled the jeans, top and underwear out of the drawer and found a hoodie tucked behind a few t-shirts. With these in hand I turned the light back out and headed for the bathroom. I left the light off, there were windows here and the light coming in from the outside was enough to see what I needed. A towel was hanging on the towel rack, and I sat my clothes on the counter.

The shower made me feel more human and got rid of the lingering smoke smell in my hair. After I got dressed, I took the clothes down to the laundry room. I dumped them into the washing machine and hoped that there was some food in the fridge that wasn't outdated. I don't know why I was bothering to wash the clothes I'd stolen. After all it didn't matter to anyone. I wasn't going to wear them again, but my mind seemed to have stuck itself on autopilot again. There wasn't much in the fridge other than a couple beers and some baking soda. Digging through the cupboards provided lots of bad for me snack foods. Apparently, Jim didn't do much cooking for himself. I took the food upstairs and sat in the chair while I ate.

Jim used to keep a small stash of cash somewhere in the house. Annie had complained about his concern about what could happen if the ATMs and debit machines went down. Even for a day they wouldn't have been able to purchase food. For more than one day there would be chaos. Annie had thought Jim was crazy. Now I was glad for his forethought. I'd be able to pull the hoodie over my head and go buy food. It would have to wait until the sun was setting. I didn't want lots of people seeing me. I had passed a corner store that looked like it would have some basics. I'd get enough for a couple of days and avoid being visible during the daylight hours. It meant that I'd have to find a good time to close the upstairs blinds. There was no tv in the guest room. With the living room being redone it meant the only way to keep up with what was happening in the world would be on the tv in the master suite. That would be noticed by anyone standing outside unless I closed the blinds. I'd wait till the middle of the night. That way there was almost no chance anyone would see. Someone may notice eventually but often people forgot what was open and closed from day to day. I sat the food on a little side table that I think Jim had put there for this express purpose. Then I crawled into his bed and fell asleep.

8

JIM

I woke to the sunset coloring the blue grey walls an odd soft purple tone. I loved it. Slowly I rose and shifted back to the chair to munch on the leftover food. It wasn't filling enough but it would hold me till I could get to the corner store. I needed to find Jim's cash stash first. Where is the one place that Annie would never look? After all she complained about it which means she knew it existed, but if she knew where it was, she'd have just spent it all and never mentioned it in the first place. I began in the closet and dug through all the drawers, then I worked my way out of the room. It was down in his office that I found it. Tucked away inside a picture of him and I after his divorce. We'd gone to a restaurant with Andy, all of us had been working late that day and were hungry. While we were there Jim had gotten Andy to take a picture of us. I'd had no idea that he'd had it framed. It was sitting on his desk, when I'd picked it up the back of the frame had come apart. There was a couple of hundred in fifties behind it. After thinking about it for a moment I decided to look behind every picture frame in the house. The only ones with money in them were the ones with him and I in them. By the end of gathering it all up, I had a couple grand in cash. That would be enough if I was careful. I could get food and move to a safe place if this one became compromised.

When night fell, I slipped out the back door and retraced my steps to the corner of the block. I could see the police car had changed. There were still people standing outside of the house with cameras reporting. Pulling the hood further down over my face I walked towards the corner store. It was only around three blocks away. As I stepped inside, I could see a tv on behind the counter. It was tuned into the news station. They were reporting that I had gone missing again and was being presumed dead. Jim was recovering. The house was a total loss. The images they were showing of the lot where my house had been located was depressing. I'd spent so much time getting that house perfect. Now I didn't know where I'd live. I was sure Lynn would take me in, even my parents or Jim would be happy to have me stay. It just wouldn't be the same. Even if I was able to rebuild it wouldn't be the same. The memories would change.

I wandered around not really paying much attention to what I was grabbing. I filled the basket and went to the front. The cashier eyed me for a moment before beginning to ring me through.

"Sad thing – that poor girl. A skull tattoo, then kidnapping and now a fire that would have left her homeless. If she were still alive. I have my doubts that she made it out of the hospital.

The Government won't let people just survive a skull like that." The kid had to be no more than eighteen or nineteen. I agreed with him just to keep him from paying too much attention to me. "Movie night tonight?"

"Yeah – my boyfriend asked for some odd things, but I just can't say no to him. You know what I mean?" The kid had scanned some microwave popcorn through when he asked. I thought saying I was meeting my boyfriend would help to keep him from thinking too much about me after I left. After all the best way to blend in was to not pretend you were trying to. I paid for the food, grabbed my bags and began the walk back.

When I got to the corner it looked like the cameras were leaving for the night.

The Target

I had one honk at me to get out of their way when I crossed the street at the stop sign. I just kept walking. They pulled up to the same street I was on and had slowed down almost as if they were looking to see who I was. I turned my back on them and went through the gate. I heard them speed off; they must have assumed I was going in the backyard of the corner house. Foolish of them to make such assumptions. I picked up my pace and was nearly taking the alley at a run when I got to Jim's back gate.

The gate didn't slam closed, but it was close. I went into the house and began putting things away. I didn't turn on any of the lights. It would have tipped people off that someone was here. I was able to make some food in the dark, but I winced every time I had to open the fridge and the light went on. I went up to the bedroom and settled in the chair again. It was close to midnight when I moved to look out the window. The street was entirely empty. I closed the curtains and put the tv on.

I was able to catch up on the investigation. I felt bad for Andrews and Dutch it looked like neither of them had slept in days. Jim was sitting in a wheelchair with Mr. Allers next to him. He looked completely defeated. They were going to let him come home tomorrow. Since no one knew where I was let alone if I was alive, they had no reason to put him into the safe house. He was going to get quite a surprise when he got home. I didn't even want Allers to know that I was living here. He was a good lawyer; he was just too pushy for me. I kept getting the feeling that he was in this for the prestige not because I had been attacked and nearly killed before. It was a relief to think that soon I wouldn't be alone.

I finished eating and took everything back to the kitchen. Washing dishes helped me not think about anything and just let my mind rest. I had forgotten the laundry in the washer. It smelled funny so I put the load back on. There wasn't too much of the night left by the time I was finished. I went back up to the bedroom and laid down. I'd left the tv on a comedy channel and an old sitcom that I liked was running. I could feel my brain shutting down. I closed my eyes so I could just listen to the show.

It was full daylight out when I woke,

the sound of a door downstairs slamming tipped me off that someone was here. I popped out of bed, shut off the tv and quietly ran into the closet. I crouched next to the door which I'd left cracked open.

"Damn useless alarm system! I know I set you when I left! Why the fuck aren't you working?!" Jim seemed overly angry at the alarm system. I was going to come out of my hiding place when I heard a second voice answer him.

"If you check the records, you can see if it actually triggered when you set it." It sounded like Mr. Allers. I slowly sat down on the floor. I'd have to wait until he left to let Jim know I was here.

"It triggered. Then a little over a day ago it was turned off. I'll have to boot my computer and dig through the biometrics access files to see who came and left. Then I can give them a piece of my mind for not setting the alarm!"

"Well if there is anything else I can do for you please don't hesitate to call me. I need to get back to my home and clean up so I can head into the office. The police are continuing to search for Ms. Hobbes. I will go down there and see if there's been any progress." There was the sound of a door opening and closing after that. I could hear Jim moving around downstairs muttering to himself about things not looking right.

I pulled myself up and slipped out of the room. At the top of the stairs, I heard Jim start to cuss again as he discovered the picture in his office had been opened and the money removed. I have a twisted sense of humor – instead of going down and easing his temper I sat on the top of the stairs and listened as Jim ran around the downstairs pulling frames apart and getting louder and angrier as he discovered that every bill he'd hidden was gone. I started to laugh. Loud. Jim came flying over to the stairs red-faced and holding his old baseball bat ready for a fight.

The look on his face when he saw me sitting there was priceless. He dropped the bat and then fell over his own feet as he tried to climb up the stairs. I stood and stepped down to him while still giggling. I was able to wrap my arms around his neck as he began to get to his feet again. For the first time since I had declined him in college, he kissed me. I didn't pull away. We stood there for what seemed like an eternity. When the kiss ended, I could feel dampness on my cheeks.

Jim was crying. He held me close to him. Then he pulled me away and gave me a little shake before pulling me back into his arms. He hadn't been able to speak a clear word since he'd seen me. He scooped me up and carried me into the bedroom and climbed on the bed. We laid there for a long time while he gathered himself.

"Where have you been and why did you run away from the hospital?" his voice hoarse from all the crying.

"I wasn't sure it was a real hospital; the doctor was too chatty; I didn't know where you were. And I think perhaps I was a little paranoid, so I made the decision to leave. I slipped out of my room, found some clothes and got out of there. I walked here and used the back entry since your house seems to be under constant coverage by the media. I tried to only do things at night once I was sure the street was empty and basically laid in bed the rest of the time. Last night I was able to close the drapes and put the tv on with no one noticing. I figured this was the safest place to be."

"How did you know where to find the cash I had hidden?"

"Annie told me about your habit of creating little cash stashes. I just went looking for it. Once I found the money behind the picture of us on your desk I figured you probably had more in the other frames. I used a little to buy food since you had nothing in the fridge."

"Yeah – I cleaned it out before coming to your place. I'm sorry about your house. It was so warm and inviting. But you can always rebuild."

"I don't know. Until this is all over, I'm not sure I want to rebuild. It could be years of dealing with the fall out. I won't be safe living alone till then."

"You're always welcome here."

"I know – that's why I came."

"Why didn't you come out when Allers was here?"

"No one can know where I am. Only you. I can't trust anyone else – everyone seems to have their own agenda."

"That's certainly a change, you've always given everyone the benefit of the doubt."

"Lesson learned, I guess. For now, I need to take some time. Andrews and Dutch are trustworthy, but I have the feeling that the police will force me into their safe house after all this. I don't trust the rest of them. Then Allers would try to do the same."

"So, we tell no one." Jim sighed heavily. "I spoke with Andrews and Dutch – the call they got about your kidnapping wasn't from a man. Some woman had been in the area when you were escorted into the building. It took her a day to realize what she had seen. She had to sober up first."

"Huh. No bodies were found around the area either – it would have been all over the news coverage. Who was the man that said he would help me then?"

"No telling now. We'll just have to

wait and see what happens next. I didn't really sleep in the hospital. Would you mind if we just crashed?"

"I don't mind." It was less than five minutes later that Jim began to snore in my ear. I nudged him on to his side and let my mind wander over the man that had said he'd help me back in the lab. His existence made no sense to me. Where did he come from? Where did he go? I don't know how long I wrestled with those thoughts but eventually my brain quieted, and I fell asleep.

* * * * *

We were able to live off the food I'd gotten for a couple of days. I did everything I could to keep out of sight of the windows. Jim would work in the living room during the day. The media would show up every morning and film the house. At night there was a space of time when there'd be no one. The new plan was going smoothly.

Jim went and took more cash out of the bank to both refill his hiding places and in case I needed to run. We knew that eventually someone would figure out I was here. Andrews and Dutch kept Jim appraised of what was happening with the case. On the third day of Jim being home they showed up on the doorstep. They were led into the living room.

"Changing things up?" Andrews seemed to like stating the obvious.

"Yeah – Annie was the one who

picked everything out. Except the office. That was the only room I was allowed to do when we got this place."

"New color looks good. There's been no change in the case. The thing is we were able to get the security camera footage from the hospital and the CCTV footage from around town the night Dawn disappeared."

"What's on there?"

"It looks like she managed to get into the lost and found, change clothes, and get out of the area. We're still filtering through the footage from town tracking her movements. The good news is that she left alone. No one took her. We'll find her eventually."

"Wait here a minute." Jim left them to their own devices and came to the stairway. I was sitting at the top. He made a little gesture at me, clearly wanting to tell them I was here but leaving it up to me to make the decision. I stood and came down the stairs. Jim draped an arm around me and began to whisper in my ear, "it'll be ok. They won't tell anyone you're here. Maybe they'll even find and keep the tapes of your path here to themselves."

"I hope so." I didn't feel very confident.

"We could argue that this is a safe house. After all no one knows you're here and we can prove that for days you've been safe. We'll just try and get them to see it's better to keep this quiet." We came around the dining room corner and face to face with Dutch first.

"Well, I'll be damned." Dutch began to shake his head as if he couldn't believe what he was seeing.

"I should have known to come and search here first. You're a heck of a lady, Dawn." Andrews seemed a little mad at himself for not thinking of checking Jim's place.

"To be fair this place has been under surveillance of some kind since before I left the hospital. I've been using the back way in and out which is all gated and doesn't look like access to this house. I kept as low a profile as I could while I've been here, coming out only at night and staying away from the windows."

"Well done! Most people aren't capable of keeping a low profile." Andrews became ridiculously proud of what I had accomplished. Dutch started to laugh quietly still not believing what he was seeing and hearing.

"We think it best that you do not tell anyone where Dawn is. This house can't be accessed unless I allow it. There's proof we can keep here safe here. I don't think it's a good idea to move her yet." Jim was adamant as he tried to explain to Andrews and Dutch what he felt.

"I'm sorry Jim but we need to get her somewhere safer. Someone is going to find her here eventually. You're the only person in town right now that she can go to. We have police presence outside her family's homes but with them out of town on that vacation the logical thing for her would be to come to you. It's not safe." Dutch looked at

Andrews as he spoke, it was clear that neither of them believed I'd be any safer in police custody but were required to do their job.

"We have to call this in." Dutch pulled his phone out of his pocket and moved into the dining room to make the call that would end the search.

I felt like I'd been hit in the stomach. They'd have found me here once they went through all the CCTV footage, but I'd have been able to move on before then if I hadn't trusted Andrews and Dutch to help. Once again, I trusted someone only to end up disappointed in the results. Dutch came back in the room as he hung up.

"A van is on its way along with some decoys. The plan is to park one by that side street gate and take her out the back way. Grafton will act as decoy. She can come through the back and swap into some street clothes. We can cover her face and put her in one of the vans out front. Then we can get out of here. The van we put Dawn in goes to the safe house and the one with Grafton will head for the station. With a little luck the media will follow that one."

There was nothing left to do. I gathered a little food to take with me since I didn't know what I'd be walking into with the safe house. I grabbed Jim's hoodie and pulled it on. I didn't want anyone to see my face. Jim had followed me up to the bedroom.

"I'm sorry. I really thought that they'd help us." He came up behind me and wrapped his arms around me burying his face in the top of my head.

"They would have if they could have. Right now, they are just trying to do their job. The van thing is going to go wrong. Someone is going to see that van on the side street. It's not like these vehicles are subtle. They'll follow and I'll be back to figuring out what to do to be safe. I'll try to make my way back here, but I have a feeling that this is where they'll look first next time."

"No – don't come back here. Take the cash and rent a room somewhere. I know you don't have any ID right now, but I know a guy. I'll get you a fake one. That should help. Stay with the safe house for a day then skip out. I can meet you at the statue by the wharf. The one where we used to get those tasty hot dogs that Annie refused to eat since it was from a food truck. We can go from there."

"Agreed." I felt better for having a plan that would lead to safety. We went back down to the living room. Andrews and Dutch had me put on a bullet proof vest under the hoodie. Then it was just a matter of waiting.

A knock on the glass door announced that Grafton had arrived. She was easily a foot taller than me. Her hair was too dark – a lovely shade of shiny black. A tattoo on her face spoke to her Mexican heritage. It was only on one side of her face; the decorations echoed a sugar skull following the lines of her face where the bone structure was. Not a skull but close. After a brief introduction she was led to the powder room where she changed and used makeup to hide the markings on her face. I knew it wouldn't work.

As soon as everyone was ready, I followed Dutch to the back door. I was able to give Jim a hug. He gave me an extra squeeze before letting go. I was escorted to the back gate. Just when I hoped we might actually pull it off I heard a buzzing overhead and looked up. There above me was a drone with a camera pointed at my face. It was like no one else saw it. I put my head down and pulled the hoodie up tighter. We went under the trees and down the alley. I was put into the unmarked van that was very obviously a police vehicle. We pulled out and started at a reasonable speed but as we drove our van began to slow down. I could only see a narrow area out of the front window. Media vans were blocking our path. Suddenly there was gunfire outside.

Dutch pushed me down for safety. I caught a glimpse of people running around outside the front of the van before I hit the floor. Suddenly the side door opened and men in masks fired on everyone. I was grabbed and hauled out of the van – there was another vehicle that had pulled up next to the door and I was shoved into the front seat.

Looking next to me I saw Agent Two. He grabbed my arm and pulled me close. A pinch told me that I was being drugged…... again! This could not be happening!

"I'm sorry Dawn."

9

SURPRISE

"We're here to keep you safe." If I heard that from one more person I was going to scream. Brogan had said it when he had pulled me into his version of a safe house. Then there had been that creepy doctor husband of his. The guys that claimed they were government officials and turned out to be from the pharmaceutical company had said the same thing. Those guys had refused to give me their names. Now here was another stranger expecting me to trust him. It wasn't even Agent Two. This guy had been sitting here for who knows how long waiting for me to wake up.

"Sure, I believe that! What are you getting out of this? I know the truth; they all just wanted me for their own use. What makes you any different?" The chair was hard and uncomfortable beneath me. The bruises from being hauled out of the van were causing me severe discomfort.

"You want to know what the target means? Why you received it? That was us. We are an unnamed group that gives people their fate. Only a small percentage of people don't follow along. Most of them are eliminated. But you – you resisted in a spectacular fashion! We ran a few tests while you were sedated. You have the potential to be one of us."

"Right. One of you. Who are you? I get the unnamed thing, but you must have a name I can call you."

"Oh yeah – you can call me Dustin. I'll be your coordinator while you work with The Group." So, this supposed unnamed group actually had a name, The Group. Now that I had my wits about me, I could see my coordinator was around my age. He had short, dirty blonde, cropped tight to his scalp hair. It clashed with his deeply tanned skin. Thin, almost non-existent lips continued to move as he spoke – I just wasn't listening.

"Ok, Dustin. I have some very specific questions. First: where am I?" There was only one door in the room. I'd have to go through him to get to it. A mirror on one side was likely two way. There was a little intercom box one of side of the mirror near the door.

"In our facility. We need to be sure you'll join us before we can show you anything further."

"If I choose not to?"

"Then I step out of this room, and you will be eliminated. We can't have you roaming free making a mess of the society we've created." I felt like I'd been poleaxed.

"Okay, nice to meet you, glad to be on board." What else was there to say? No thanks I'd rather be terminated? Not likely. Looks like stepping back from work in the company had been the right decision. I wouldn't be able to do both jobs.

"Happy to make the offer. There's some paperwork that you'll have to sign. Some standard NDAs. Also, we will need to start erasing your existence from history. I know – it sounds a little odd but there's a whole process. I'll show it to you when it's time to start. In fact, it'll be one of the first exercises you do with the nano equipment we give you. That and removal of your target."

"It'll be nice to not be on everyone's radar. I can visit with my nephew and the rest of my family with no one following me." There was a sense of relief knowing I wouldn't be putting anyone I love in danger.

"Oh. Well, that's one of the things we will explain. When we erase you, we start with all the people that have heard of you and then work back to people that know you personally. Those are harder to do; we have some special nano bots we use for them. It's based on brainwashing. It senses when you appear in the persons mind, using their brain chemistry, then alters the chemical signature to leave the feelings but remove the memory. Eventually they stop thinking of you and just have the feelings. You will never have to deal with your family again."

Dustin seemed thrilled with his pronouncement. I, however, loved my family and wanted them to remember me. Given the fact that my face had been everywhere through world news, I knew it would take some time to erase me. That would give me the time

I needed to get out of this. We walked through what felt like miles of hallways. Dustin kept pointing out different rooms. That was the well-appointed exercise space, that's where the meal hall was. One of the creators had been a famous chef and so we had restaurant quality meals coming out of there. We went through a large fire door that led to the living areas. He gave a long explanation on how we had the best of everything. The newest technology, the cleanest tech that wasn't even on the market yet. This was mainly because they had bought the patents to suppress the existence of life changing gizmos.

Everything looked very expensive here. All of it provided so you had luxury comforts….. so long as you went along with the program.

Eventually we reached our destination and I was left alone on a super soft and fluffy chaise lounge while Dustin retrieved the paperwork. I dozed off and woke hours later. There was a note on the coffee table. Apparently, this extravagant apartment was mine. It stated that the sedative would take time to get out of my system and I should rest as much as I wanted. If there was anything I needed to just dial 599 on the intercom and he would be there to help. Once I had signed the paperwork we would discuss when to start my training. I wondered how long I could stay in this place before they began to wonder about said paperwork.

I slowly wandered around and learned where everything was in my apartment. On the first floor I had a large lounging area that could be considered a formal living room, on the far side were some large windows that overlooked a greenspace. There was also a door that led to a large balcony. When I stepped out, I was able to count that I was a good fifteen floors up. Beyond the green space was a beach. I could hear the ocean waves coming on shore and smell the salt in the air. It was sunny and humid. There was another balcony above mine that provided some shade, making this area very pleasant.

Back inside I turned to my right and found a small tv area hiding behind a wall. Next to this was a large dining room that contained a massive table that could have easily fit forty people without having anyone's elbows touch. A glass wall beyond that gave a glimpse of the kitchen. I walked in and found that it was fully stocked. Not only with the kinds of food that I normally would find at the grocery store but also with exotic items I'd never seen before. The mess hall would be nice when I didn't feel like cooking, but this kitchen made my old one feel miniscule. All kinds of equipment stood on the counters and in little appliance garages, things you see on specialty cooking shows and cooking competitions. On the far side of the main room, I could see a large fireplace with a little seating area around it. A door to one side led to a large powder room. There were two sets of stairs – one that went up above the kitchen and to the left and one that went up next to the powder room door and to the right. I followed the one next to the powder room first.

There was a single bedroom there. It was massive! It had its own seating area with a fireplace and tv mounted to the wall. A set of windows with an exterior door next to them opened to another balcony with more seating that could be made private by pulling some curtains on either side. The walk-in closet was already filled with clothes. All of them looked like they had been tailored to fit me. There was everything a girl could want – from loose fitting comfy sweats and legging, to hoodies, to fancy ballroom gowns that looked like they had been based on Disney princess outfits. Shoes from every major designer were there and in my size. Multiples of each item to give me colour choices, and at least fifty pairs of slippers as well. Next to the closet was a bathroom that belonged in a spa. It had a walk-in shower with a seat if I wanted. The water and jets looked like they would spray every inch of me easily without missing any spots. Then there was a space where you could lay down and have it rain on you.

The bathtubs were spectacular. Yes bathtubs, plural, as in more than one. There was one that was a clawfoot soaker, one that was modern and had jets, then one that opened from the side and had a seat in it with jets as well. The last one had a spot for aroma therapy and what looked like LED lights in it. The counter here was large and had a deep sink. An entire section was set up as a vanity with specialty lighting around the mirror and brand name makeup already chosen and laid out in unique containers for me. The overhead lights were on a dimmer switch.

I went back out and looked at the bed. There was no mistaking the bed size, I'd seen the 12-foot designs on the internet and thought that it was odd. In this room it looked like it was a regular king-sized bed. The only reason I could tell the difference was because I walked around it and there was no way it was a normal size. It was very overwhelming. At the same time, I wanted to climb up and start jumping since there was no way for me to actually fall off the bed as long as I stuck to the center.

Heading back down the stairs I crossed the formal living room and went up the stairs by the kitchen. At the top was a single door. I opened it and there was a chair in the center of the room surrounded by screen and control panels. This must be where I would do my work. I left the workroom and slowly closed the door behind me. I needed to eat something. I was beginning to feel nauseous. When I looked around the kitchen there were five kinds of bread ready and waiting to make a sandwich. Forty different kinds of cheese and every kind of milk you could think of as well.

All I wanted was something simple. My go to grilled cheese and some chips would be fine. I got everything ready quickly. I found a fancy root beer in the fridge and decided I would sit outside. I placed everything on the balcony table and settled myself on the couch that was there. Looking around I couldn't see into anyone else's balcony. There were no sounds of traffic. No sounds of people talking.

Just the ocean waves. Slowly I ate and drank. Then I dozed off again.

When I woke it was dark out. It had gotten cooler but not cold. The breeze had died down. I carried my things back inside and placed the dishes in the dishwasher. There, still sitting where I'd left them earlier, were the papers. I should read them before I sign them. It would take a couple of days. There were a lot of them. It wasn't until I was thirty pages in that I found something that could be useful to me. It stated that once you became a field agent you could go anywhere and do anything you wanted. It then detailed the process for becoming a field agent. It would take months, but I knew that it was going to be my way out. On page one hundred I turned in for the night.

The Target

* * * * *

All I could think when I woke up was how badly I needed a wash. I could smell myself. I slept on the side of the bed closest to the bathroom just in case I needed it during the night. Now entering the walk-in closet, I was happy for all the options. I found a pair of leggings that were soft and in dark chocolate brown tones. I pulled out a shirt and hoodie both in greens then headed for the shower.

It was like standing under a waterfall in a jungle. The water was the perfect warm temperature. A selection of soaps, shampoos and conditioners made choosing what to try difficult. I ended up with an apple blossom scent. I scrubbed up thoroughly and dried off.

I felt invigorated. Once I was dressed, I grabbed the paperwork and began the trek out of the apartment area to find the mess hall. I got turned around a couple of times and had no idea where I was. Finally, I gave up wandering and knocked on a door. Someone would give me directions.

Agent Two opened it. I had no idea how this could have happened. Of all the locations I could have picked it was the one that held the only other person I vaguely knew. He stood there staring at me for a moment before opening his door further and gesturing with his head for me to come in.

"I didn't think you'd come to see me this quickly," I was able to get a good look him finally. His black hair was still the same length but instead of being in a military style it had grown out a little and now seemed to sit on his forehead more, softening how he looked. With the sunglasses gone I could see his eyes were a warm brown. His lips looked much fuller than they had previously. His skin was an olive tone. Now that he was out of his suit, I could see that he must work out – he was heavily muscled. I stepped into his apartment.

"What's your name?" I was done with not knowing who I was speaking with.

"Rodrigo."

"Honestly, I wasn't looking for you. I was trying to find the mess hall."

"Come and sit. I'll make you something. If you have any questions, feel free to ask." I followed him into his kitchen and sat at the island bar space. He wandered around pulling things out of his fridge and cupboard before settling it all next to the cooktop on the island.

"Why did you not help me out of the pharmaceutical company's testing site?"

"Actually, I did. I needed to observe you closely to make sure you could become one of us. After I was shown out, they tried to shoot me. That was a mistake on their part. I called in backup and one of the guys on the team called the cops to get you out of there. We have people that can walk in and out of any police precinct around the world. If you'd taken them up on the safe house, we would have brought you here much sooner." He deftly picked up some burger, made it into a round and placed it on to the frying pan.

"Are you the ones that burned down my house?"

"No. When you get to page 130, you'll see that you sign over all assets to The Group. In turn they use it to make money for this place. My grandfather was one of the people that started the pager trend with all profits funneled here. We had cell phones a decade before anyone else. We had laptops in the seventies. That's what the money does."

"Then if I'd stayed at the hospital, you would have come and gotten me from there too. That makes sense. You're a field agent, right? What's it like? What are the benefits?" I was finally able to ask the questions I wanted answered. I could know for sure if my slowly forming plan would work.

"I like it. There's lots of training and special equipment that you need to get the hang of using. My favorite part is being able to flag people like you, the ones with potential. I have no family left – my grandfather was the only person I had and he's long dead – each person I bring into the group is someone that I feel could be part of my family here. If you're interested, then I can introduce you to some people once you've signed off on your paperwork. Until you sign, you're still an outsider." He flipped the burgers like an expert and began to toast the buns.

"I think that may be the direction I go. Field work. I'm still reading through everything, but it sounds like you have more freedom to do things in the field."

Rodrigo served the burgers and chips.

While we ate, I continued to read the paperwork. He simply observed me. I felt awkward. Being looked at made me feel weird at the best of times and caused me to be clumsy at the worst of times. Inevitably I spilled mustard on my hoodie. I made my excuses and he offered to take me back to my apartment. Once there he showed me where the map of the facility was – hiding in a drawer of the coffee table.

I managed to read the entire contract by the end of the day. I knew I had no choice. I signed it. Dialing the number that Dustin had left, the intercom crackled to life. I informed him I had signed the contract but that I still felt exhausted and would appreciate having a couple days to recover before I began my training.

The Target

* * * * *

A week later I was sitting in my control room with Dustin in a chair behind me. I had begun to erase my memory from the list of people that had heard of me. Thanks to the news and the internet there were hundreds of millions of names on this list. The procedure itself was not difficult. Carefully I would locate a person in the database that had any knowledge of me. I would select the information I wanted deleted. Then I pressed the button and nanobots did the rest. It would take years to get to my family and in the meantime, they were still looking for me. I'd seen the news on tv. Lynn had put some of her ex-husband's money up as a reward for information.

"Don't worry about the reward. We've taken some steps, so you won't be on the news circuit anymore." It was a reassurance that was wearing thin. I would spend four hours every morning working through the list. Each day I got a little more efficient at the process and was able to get through more names. The afternoons were dedicated to training for the field. It was going to be months before I could leave and put my skills into practice.

"I'm just focusing. I always feel fumble fingered when someone watches me type or do any kind of work. Taking extra care to do things slows me down."

"Well then, you'll be relieved to hear that I'm clearing you to do this on your own from here on. We will continue meeting in the afternoons for field training. Though to be honest you pick things up so quickly I doubt you'll have more than another week of training before you're ready there as well." Dustin seemed a little sad that I was picking things up so quickly.

"Once I finish field training does it mean I can start taking assignments?"

"Yes. Though you need to get through far more names on that list before you can leave the compound. You can't be recognized out there. Once we clear enough names, I'll let you know."

"You seem a little sad that I've picked this up so fast. I thought you would be happy – after all it proves that I do have the potential."

"It means I have to move on to another person that needs additional training. I find spending time with you enjoyable.

I don't want it to end. Would you consider hanging out with me after we're done your training?"

"Well, I don't really know anyone else here so yeah – it'd be nice to make some friends."

"You should try looking at the common room. I think they are hosting horror nights for the next couple weeks. Everyone shows up around 2 and it runs till the early hours in the morning. Now that I've given you a pass and your afternoon training is more of a practice thing, you can determine when and where you work. There's no real worry. Do things at your own pace. Figure out when you want days off. That kind of thing."

"Thanks, I will look at that. I haven't really watched horror movies since I was a teenager. My friends in college didn't like them and I just did everything I could to fit in with them." I didn't want Dustin to know that I was having dinners regularly with Rodrigo and his 'family'. Most of them were too young for me to relate to. I did my best, but they didn't feel like real friends, and I had a family.

Dustin left at 1:30 that day. I was able to go and clean up before pulling out the map. I followed it down to the common room and made it just in time to get some popcorn and a soda. Rodrigo spotted me and waved me over to sit with him. I looked around and couldn't see Dustin anywhere.

"Hey, I didn't know you liked horror movies. Todays is a good one: Halloween Kills." Rodrigo seemed pleased that I had chosen to sit with him.

"It's been a long time since I watched horror. I'm glad that you're here. If I get too scared, I can lean on you." The idea that I'd get too scared seemed to please Rodrigo, or perhaps it was the thought of me leaning on him that made him smile.

I ended up curling into Rodrigo's side several times throughout the movie. He slid his arm around my shoulders and let me hide my face in his shoulder during the worst spots. We ended up sharing the popcorn and soda that I had brought in. After the movie finished, I felt Rodrigo stretch next to me, he grabbed my hand and pulled me to my feet. He didn't let go as he led me out of the common room. I found his touch oddly comforting. We went down a hall that I had never noticed before. At the end we stepped into a glass room filled with plants.

"I know you can't leave the compound and there's only so much you can do on those balconies. You won't find people in here much after 3pm. It's marked as the solarium on the map but if you go through that door on the far left you're in the garden that keeps the facility fed. At least the one that they let the gardening inclined residents use. All the trees are fruits and you're free to take whatever you want."

"Thank you for showing me this. I'm not getting anywhere near enough time with plants these days. I used to love to garden at my house. I ripped out the backyard and put nothing but plants and fruit trees in."

"I know. It's one of the reasons I

brought you here. Plus, they were going to show the movie Babadook next, and I don't think that you would have enjoyed that one. If you want to come tomorrow afternoon, I can meet you. It's going to be Halloween Ends." There was a little twinkle in Rodrigo's eye when he mentioned coming to the horror movies the next afternoon.

"I think I can do that. Do they ever do something that isn't horror related?"

"They do holiday screenings. With Easter coming up next month we'll be inundated with those. After that they will make different selections – usually one week each month. Once October hits you get all the Halloween stuff for a month. Then in November you get the Christmas stuff until January."

"No Thanksgiving?"

"Nope. We don't celebrate that here. Follow me – I'll show you where to find the library. There's a book you should read." We exited the solarium and walked back past the common room. It was several corridors before we arrived. When we walked in, I could smell the books, the dust and sunshine. Here the building was five or six stories high with stairs to different levels. I followed Rodrigo through to the back of the room and up two levels before he turned down a set of shelves. There at the back under a window on a little podium was a very large and heavy-looking book. From the smell and the delicacy of the pages it had to be very old.

"What is this?"

"The real history of the world. As written by The Group. The ones that control everything. How we were formed. It was longer ago than you may believe. This version is a translation to English that started thousands of years ago. There's a copy that was translated to modern English, I have it up in my apartment. Go there when you're ready to learn the truth about life." Rodrigo left me there staring at the page that was open.

I read the first line of the page repeatedly, "We are the creators. We are the ones who tell society what is and isn't acceptable. Anyone who gets in our way will be eliminated."

My brain wouldn't let me read any further. I turned and slowly navigated my way back to my apartment. I climbed into a bath and turned on the jets. I didn't want to be here anymore. That single line in the book explained the entire structure of our world. Those behind the scenes had made society what it is. There was nothing anyone out there could do to change what they decided. Change could only come from within.

10

SHADOWS

I couldn't think for weeks. The mornings were filled with me removing myself from the minds of people. I was taught to remove the target from my arm. The news slowly stopped airing any mention of my name. I had finished my field training and passed the final practice. Dustin would show up a couple times a week just to hang out while I did my work. He would make lunch for us. I never asked him to stay, or to come back.

There was more I needed to know. I needed information - the real history. I decided to go and see Rodrigo the next morning. Take a day off working. A day to sleep late and eat anything I wanted. I made a sandwich for dinner and curled up on my balcony. Sleep seemed to evade me. When it hit midnight and I still couldn't get to sleep I went out into the hall and began the quiet trek to Rodrigo's place.

I had passed people in the halls here – they were rarely empty. Tonight though, they weren't only empty, they were silent. The kind of silence that is oppressive and causes your skin to tingle as if you're hypersensitive to the air. At first, I tried to breath quietly so

I wouldn't accidentally wake anyone but then it felt like someone was following me and I didn't want them to hear where I was. There was acute relief when I made it to my destination. I knocked as quietly as I could while still making it so my knock could be heard.

Rodrigo opened the door and stepped back to let me in without saying a word. He was only wearing a pair of pajama pants. I walked over to his coffee table and picked up the book. Turning to leave I felt him grab me from behind to stop me. His breath was warm against my ear as he spoke.

"You can stay if you want. From the looks of you, you've been spending too much time in the control room. Haven't been able to sleep, eh?"

"No. I've tried but since you showed me that book, I haven't been able to sleep at all. It was disturbing."

"Lay on the couch. Rest and read. Take your time. You are always welcome in my home." Rodrigo nudged me to his couch. I settled down and began reading. He pulled a blanket over me.

When I woke up the book was on the floor and there was a tray of food on the coffee table with a note. I picked up the book and swung my legs over the edge of the couch. There was a selection of pastries and a mini jug of orange juice with a cup. Picking up the note I began to eat and read.

Dawn,

Take as much time as you need. My home is yours. Take the book with you and return it when you are done. Whatever makes you feel better. Under this note is a key to access my apartment. I took an assignment and will be away for a few weeks. Don't go watching any scary movies until I return to protect you from them, ok?

R.

Sitting next to the tray was the key. Somehow, I had been 'keyed' and by a man that I barely knew. It was an odd feeling. His apartment was just as luxurious as mine. With all the same amenities. The only difference is that no one would know I was here. A haven from Dustin and the rest of The Group within their walls.

I did the dishes and cleaned up the apartment. It was only fair since I'd stayed here. Taking the key and book I went back to my apartment only to find the door cracked open. Standing in my living room was Dustin with a handful of red roses.

"Hey, I brought you some flowers. I couldn't find you though, where were you hiding?"

"I couldn't sleep so I went down to the library and started looking through books. I found one that I thought would be a good read. Just coming back in. How did you get in my apartment? I thought that I locked it."

"Oh, I have a copy of the key – every coordinator has a copy of the key to his apprentice's home. Normally I would have turned it in, but I thought since we've been getting close that I'd hang on to it."

"Ah – I see. Ok, let me just run up and put some clothes on and drop this book up by my bed." I was suddenly feeling like I needed to start sleeping elsewhere. Dustin was giving me creeper vibes. I'm glad that Rodrigo had given me a key. Picking the loosest and least attractive clothes I could find I began hunting for a safe spot to keep the key. In a bathroom drawer that I hadn't really dug through I found a simple chain that resembled dog tags. I opened it and slid the key down. There was no way I was going to leave it where Dustin would have the opportunity to find it if he started snooping. He was still waiting for me when I came downstairs.

"Since it looks like you haven't eaten

breakfast I went ahead and ordered us some delivery. I hope you like steak and eggs."

I hated eggs. Baked into food I didn't care but cooked/fried eggs didn't taste right to me. When they arrived instead of going out on the balcony, he had them taken right into the dining room and placed at either end of the giant table. We then sat in silence while we ate. The steak was delicious and there were biscuits as well. I moved the eggs around on my plate to make it look like I had eaten some before tossing my napkin on top of the dish to hide them.

"Thank you for breakfast. I think I'm going to head up to the control room and work though."

"I'll come past later and check in on

you."

He left without offering to tidy up the mess. I took a little time to clear the plates and put the dishwasher on. Nowhere in my apartment felt safe now. I felt like eyes were on me all the time. Pretending to be calm, I went up to my control room and started clearing people from the list. If I could just get enough of them done, I could get out of here.

* * * * *

A couple of months passed. I worked every day all day and often into the night as well. Sleep eluded me most nights. The book had given me nightmares. It told how people had justified doing horrible things to alter the way society worked, until everyone was an unknowing slave to the system. They had no way out. I pushed myself harder and harder to find an escape. The trial had been pushed out since I still hadn't been found. The defense was asking for all charges to be dropped but the prosecution was trying to keep the attempted murder charges for my sister in view. Annie and Mark had both admitted to planning Lynn's murder during the time that they were actively trying to take me out.

Rodrigo wasn't back from his assignment yet. When I couldn't take it anymore, I would pack a bag and in the middle of the night each night and would move a few of my things into his apartment. Just enough to sleep comfortably. With him away I was doing all the cleaning in there. I know that once a week he had cleaners come in and at the same time they would fill his fridge. No one seemed to notice I had been sleeping there. I would sneak back home in the early hours of the morning, just in case Dustin decided he wanted to share breakfast again. The key never left me.

The control room wasn't so bad. I must admit there was a certain amount of satisfaction in removing my existence from people that I didn't like. It was odd how many people had cruel thoughts about people they didn't even know. We could see everything going on in the persons mind thanks to the nano bots. I had discovered that the bots were introduced during the vaccinations for babies. All of us had literally grown up with them in our bodies.

Once I had been removing myself from the mind of a mother who had a baby that was crying. I had gone into the baby's bot panel and found out that he had an untreated ear infection. Since no one was around I had put the thought of a possible ear infection into the mother's mind. I checked back a week later and the baby was getting treatment. Small kindnesses had to make a difference. At least I felt slightly better for helping in some small way.

Dustin entered from the side door that connected all the control pods together. He'd made it clear that he was attracted to me. People in The Group were encouraged to find matches among their peers. The more children that were born with the potential the better – a legacy they called it. I had done my best to discourage him. He had listened when I had gone on a mini rant about tans and how they needed to match the person's hair tones. Over the last few weeks his skin had lost that intense darkness that clashed with everything. I still found him creepy. I just couldn't like his true self. He presented a nice guy persona to me but the guy that I had watched in the control pod was totally different. Seeing him place a skull on the arm of a 7-year-old child had been devastating. Yet he hadn't even flinched. Just shrugged and asked if I wanted to grab a bite in the mess hall.

He set his hands on either side of the back of my chair and leaned in close to my ear, "So I've been thinking that we should do something a little different today. You've erased the memory from enough people that you can leave the compound now. Let's go out and spend a little money."

"What did you have in mind?" I couldn't help but shiver in revulsion at how close he was to me. Not to mention he had just given me the key to my way out of this place before I was forced to erase myself from my family.

"There's a chopper on the roof. Let's fly to Vancouver and get dinner and a show. I took the liberty of requisitioning you an appropriate outfit. Go see if it fits and if not call the tailor's and have them come and adjust it for you. I'll pick you up around 3."

With that he was gone. I closed my station. To one side was the box I would need to carry when I was out in the field. I pulled it into the main area of my apartment. The Group had massive amounts of nano tech – some even altered the very genetics of a person. They'd been testing that one only recently. In the box there was a little case – smaller than my clutch. The rest of the box contained refill items. I walked into my bedroom and changed. The dress fit me flawlessly. It even made me look taller when I looked in the mirror. If all went well this would be the last time I would be in this place. I slid the kit into my clutch along with as many of the refills as I could get. The special debit card they had issued me went in with some lipstick. I'd written Rodrigo a note and left it in the drawer of his bedside table. Everything was ready.

I wasn't sure how this would go down; all I knew was that I had to make my escape at the first opportunity. They couldn't track the card. That was all part of their plan. Be invisible and make as much money as you can. Take out anyone that may one day get in their way. I had to take a deep breath. It was so much more complicated now. I'd kept my list of contacts down to nothing in the building. Only Dustin and Rodrigo had much contact with me. I made all my own meals and ordered things to be delivered to the apartment during times I knew I would be working in the pod or hiding out at Rodrigo's apartment. Once I made Dustin forget what I looked like I should be able to get away from The Group. I hoped. Then I could bring as much attention to them as possible. What they did was wrong, and I couldn't leave them to continue to do evil.

Three o'clock came and with it, Dustin's arrival. He was in a very high-end suit. Again, he brought red roses. I slid them into the vase on the coffee table. When he took my arm, I could feel how cold and clammy his hands were. I hadn't really bothered looking at the floors above me when I was in the elevator. The building went up to fifty floors and then there was button labelled roof. Dustin hit that one.

When we emerged into the bright light, I could see that the building sat on an island, and you couldn't see the mainland from anywhere on this roof. There was a small mountain situated behind us on one side, you could see the outdoor gardens surrounding the building and people moving around like little ants everywhere. I began to wonder if Dustin had tried to purposely keep me inside because it was difficult to find a spouse that wasn't related to you in the compound. I was his shot at having a legacy without any possible issues from too much inbreeding.

The chopper took off and flew straight out above the ocean. No one spoke during the hour-long trip. We landed at a little island that had nothing but a landing strip, lighthouse and some exterior lighting. The chopper was refueled and took off again for another hour before the mainland came into sight. It looked like we were north of L.A. somewhere. We landed at a private airport owned by The Group where we were escorted into a Learjet that took off. A five-star restaurant meal was served while we were in the air. I was sitting in a seat across from Dustin and he tried to play footsie with me. Shifting my feet away to give him some room and to minimize contact was all I could do.

"We should only be another hour from Vancouver. I've arranged for us to see a play. Then we can get another meal followed by some clubbing." Dustin sounded a bit nervous.

"That sounds lovely."

"We won't be back to the compound until tomorrow morning, is that ok?"

"Absolutely. I haven't been around people in a long time. Clubbing especially sounds fun." It wasn't a lie.

I'd never been clubbing when I was younger – Jim, Annie and the company had taken all my time. Plus clubbing would give me the opportunity to free myself.

It wasn't long before we had arrived at another private airstrip. A limo with a driver was waiting for us. We managed to get downtown and to the theater just as they were flashing the lights to get everyone seated. Dustin walked past everyone and led me up the stairs and down a hallway. There were sets of curtains blocking various spots. We entered the one at the far end, a private box. The show was Pretty Woman the Musical.

I barely paid attention to the show as Dustin kept trying to get closer to me. First an arm around my shoulders. Keeping my shoulders straight and not letting Dustin know how uncomfortable I was, took priority. His hand tried to slide down my arm through the show. I curled a little into myself to keep him from trying anything further.

Dinner was at the Top of Vancouver Revolving restaurant. When we arrived, the entire place was empty except for the maître d', the waiters, and the kitchen staff. Dustin had reserved the entire restaurant for the night. We were served a lovely meal that I didn't even taste due to the intensity of my emotions and nerves. It felt like he was leading me down a path I'd rather not go. We barely spoke until after they had brought out the desert, a lovely tiramisu with a giant diamond ring stuck in the top of mine.

"I know we haven't been together that

long, but I just feel so connected to you and since we both have such high potential we could pair up and have excellent offspring for our legacy. Marry me."

Worst. Proposal. Ever.

All I could think was if I said no the night would be over. Now I was in a hard position. If I said yes, I had to get free tonight. Messing up would lead to me being stuck with this creep for the foreseeable future. If I said no, I'd be back at the compound with no other way out until I had completed removing myself from my family's memories.

"Yes. I will marry you." There really had been no choice. Tonight was the only shot I'd get at freedom. He'll be less likely to think I'd take off at the club if we were engaged. The ring had to be worth a fortune. I could find a place to pawn it for cash.

He looked genuinely happy as he slid the ring on to my finger. We finished eating and then climbed back into the limo. I had no idea what club we were going until we pulled up to Celebrities Night Club. There was a line up around the block. The driver stopped the limo right in front of the door and Dustin handed me out. He walked up to the bouncer and nodded at him as we passed through the door. I could hear people making comments about money as we went in.

The dance floor and every table was jam packed. Dustin went to the bar and got us a couple of drinks. I took mine and turned in a circle pretending to drink it while dumping it into a nearby glass. Everyone had to shout to be heard over the DJ's music. The flashing lights were disorienting. I needed Dustin to drink enough to not follow me when I decided to use the washroom.

Over the next half hour, I managed to dump more than ten drinks into various glasses and on the floor as we danced. He signaled me to follow him over to one of the bars.

"Enjoying the club?"

"Yes – though I think I'm going to find the washroom while you get me another drink honey." He was finally drunk enough and distracted enough to let me walk away on my own. I went down the side hall and spotted an exit near the washrooms. I went to go use the door and was stopped by a bouncer.

"I'm sorry miss but you can't leave that way."

"Look my date has been getting more and more handsy all night, he keeps trying to touch me in ways I don't like and won't listen when I tell him to stop. I need to get away from him and get in a cab before he realizes I'm gone. I told him I was going to the washroom. Is there any way out of here that is safe for me?"

"We have a code z." The bouncer spoke into his headset. "It'll be ok ma'am – when we call a code z the bartender takes an extra-long time to make the drinks and if you follow me I'll show you a side exit. We have a car service that keeps someone there for situations like this."

"Thank you." I followed the bouncer down the side hall and out the door. There was a Lyft sitting on the side of the building. The bouncer led me to the door and spoke with the driver before letting me get in the car.

"Where too?" The driver looked at me questioningly. I pulled out my phone and looked up hotels at the edge of Vancouver.

"The Westminster Best Western please."

"Wow – thanks! The club pays for these services, and you just made it so that my night is worth leaving my friends at the club! Feel free to sit back and relax. We could be a while getting there."

I pulled the ring off my finger and put it in to my clutch. Turning off the phone was a start. I'd have to find a place to ditch it and buy a burner. "Hey, any idea where near the hotel I could buy a new phone and sell an engagement ring?"

"Yeah, if you go a couple blocks up from the hotel there's a bunch of electronics shops and a couple pawn shops. You should be able to find something there."

We lapsed back into silence for the remainder of the drive. He dropped me at the front door of the hotel. The girl behind the counter looked at me in confusion when I walked in with no luggage.

"Good evening. How can I help you tonight?"

"I need a room. My boyfriend got violent. I don't have my ID. Is that ok?

I managed to get my debit card before I ran." I could only hope the explanation would strike a chord with her and she'd overlook the usual rules.

"I completely understand. We don't get this often, but we can help. You did the right thing getting out of there. You are now Miss Smith. Your room will be 509 – its right by an emergency exit just in case he figures out how to track your phone. If you prepay for the night, then we don't have to have a card on file."

"Thank you so much." I let a little quaver enter my voice while I pulled out my card. She handed me a door card and pointed me in the direction of the elevator. I rode it up and found my room. It was sparse but clean. It would be enough. After all, The Group would think that I could get any expensive hotel room I wanted. They shouldn't think I would come here. I went in the bathroom and had a quick wash before I climbed into bed. Sleep eluded me again. Watching the light on the ceiling change from artificial to natural daylight made me feel odd. I missed my family. Going back to them would cause nothing but problems. My next steps were going to be difficult. I wanted to see them, I wanted to sleep in a bed that was more comfortable than this.

There was a continental breakfast in the dining room when I got up. I ate very little and tried to hide in a corner. There wouldn't be anything on the news about my disappearance. The Group was going to hunt me themselves. Checking out took a little time and the girl gave me directions to the nearest Apple Store. The walk took over an hour because I stopped and purchased some inconspicuous clothing at a big box retail store. I felt less vulnerable once I had changed. Then I headed into the Apple store.

I selected the newest phone and created a brand-new Apple account using my middle name and the generic Smith last name. From there I walked to a pawn shop and sold the ring for several thousand dollars. Using my new phone, I looked up people selling cars for cheap, not a dealership or lot, and found one that would do. I called a cab and was able to go to a somewhat sketchy neighborhood and buy the car. With no ID I couldn't get insurance or plates. When no one was watching I took mud and smeared the back and front of the car where the plates should have been. If I stuck to back roads on my way out of the city, I shouldn't draw any attention.

It took all day to get from where I was in Burnaby, through the Brentwood area and up North Vancouver to Horseshoe Bay. Once there I had no choice but to take the Sea-to-Sky highway towards Whistler. It seemed like no one had noticed the fact that the car had mud where it shouldn't be. A couple of hours later I was in Pemberton. I ditched the car on a side road and found a Super 8 hotel. Once there I was finally able to sleep.

In the middle of the night, I could feel a burning sensation getting more and more painful on my arm. The target was back. I pulled my kit out of the clutch and removed it. The pain was agonizing. Seconds later the target was back. I wouldn't let them win. The Group had to face justice.

EPILOGUE

The mountains surrounding me were still covered in snow. I was working my way farther and farther north. I'd managed to get to the Yukon Territory in northern Canada. It was sparsely populated, and I kept moving around so that The Group wouldn't find me. I had managed to purchase a truck with a camper on the back. I'd also managed to contact a rather unscrupulous fellow and acquired fake paperwork, so I had ID, truck plates and insurance. I also used some cash to buy appropriate clothing, I stuck to long sleeves, not just to help me keep warm but to hide the target tattoo. I'd tried removing it multiple times and it had always returned. Everywhere I went I tried to educate people about the tattoos. I'd tell them it was The Group, and that you could change and choose your own fate.

When I had an opportunity, I would watch the tv's in hotels. At first there was nothing, then slowly over the course of months I began to see reports that spoke of how people were hearing about a Group. That they were really the ones giving the tattoos. How the only way things were going to change was by how we as people chose to handle the tattoos.

I pulled into the side of a Petro Can in

The Target

Stewart Crossing and parked. I climbed through the back of the truck and into my camper. A meal sounded like a good idea, and I had lots of time. The door on the camper was suddenly wrenched open and a large man jumped in.

Rodrigo had found me. We stared at each other in complete silence. He was holding a tattoo kit. I could feel a burning on my arm again. Slowly so that he wouldn't think I was trying anything I rolled my sleeve up and looked down at my arm. The target was gone. Now as I stared at the empty space a phoenix slowly grew on to the open skin. I smiled. That would be my goal. To build my life back up from the ashes the skull had left behind. I still couldn't get that four-leaf clover though, no matter how hard I tried.

The Target

Luck was still no friend of mine.

ABOUT THE AUTHOR

I still think that no one reads these sections. After all, you've just read an entire book and let's face it – who cares about the author and their own self-interest? Yes, I still love cheese. A second fact about me – I like to garden. Now here's the fancy grilled cheese recipe used in the story.

Ingredients:

For the sandwich:

French Bread 4 slices
Any fancy cheese you like – use one that's sharp and one that melts really well. Make sure to grate them.
Butter

For the sauce:

1 cup milk

1 tablespoon butter
1 tablespoon flour
1 cup cheese – half of each type from above grated.

Process:

Grate all your cheese first. Take a half cup of each and set aside for the sauce. Make sure you have enough to fill each of your sandwiches. Butter each slice of bread on one side only, be sure to get from one crust all the way to the other – this is key for good browning. Make your sauce now. Melt the butter until it just starts to brown. This gives your sauce a slightly nutty flavor (goes well with Gouda) Next, add your flour and stir until a thick paste forms. Cook this for a minute to get rid of the flour taste. Add your milk and stir with a whisk until smooth. Heat up a frying pan over medium heat – not too hot. This is a 5 or 6 on my stove but each one is different so go with what works for you. Add two pieces of the French bread butter side down into the pan. Place your grated cheese in a layer on each slice. Add the top slice and cover frying pan with a lid. This will help the butter on the other side to start melting and help the cheese to start melting as well. Next add your cheese to the sauce and turn down to low. Stir using a wooden spoon to make sure it blends well. After a couple minutes turn the heat off on the sauce and add pepper to taste. You don't need salt. There's lots of salt in the cheese and butter. Feel free to add paprika, fresh rosemary, or anything that would change up the flavor if you want. Flip the grilled cheese. If the bottom is not quiet a medium to dark brown give it a couple more minutes. Add a little bit of water to the edge of the pan (maybe a tablespoon) and cover with the lid again. Leave it for at least three minutes. Then check to see if the cheese has melted and the bottom to make sure it isn't burning. Adjust the heat to keep from burning. Once everything is ready, place the first grilled cheese on the plate then add sauce on top. Stack the second grilled cheese and drizzle more sauce there as well. Put the remaining sauce in a little ramekin and use this to dip. Goes well with a side of chips and a beer – or root beer if you don't drink or have somewhere to drive.

Next time we'll talk chocolate.

Manufactured by Amazon.ca
Bolton, ON